D0280922

SWEET VENGEANCE

Aspiring actress Kelley Robinson mistakes infatuation for love when she falls for charismatic media celebrity Carl Roche. Despite the warnings of her friends, she believes his promises and moves in with him. But when she discovers how he has deceived her, she is determined to get her revenge. Paul, a seemingly sympathetic journalist, offers to help put her plan into action. But is he only looking for a good story for his newspaper? Who can Kelley really trust?

ROBERTA GRIEVE

◆

SWEET VENGEANCE

Complete and Unabridged

LINFORD
Leicester

First published in Great Britain in 2014

First Linford Edition
published 2015

A catalogue record for this book is available
from the British Library.

ISBN 978–1–4448–2370–7

Published by
F. A. Thorpe (Publishing)
Anstey, Leicestershire

Set by Words & Graphics Ltd.
Anstey, Leicestershire
Printed and bound in Great Britain by
T. J. International Ltd., Padstow, Cornwall

This book is printed on acid-free paper

1

Heads turned as the door to Marie's Hair and Beauty crashed open and Kelley Robinson rushed in, her cheeks flushed with excitement.

Mary Winters, known to her exclusive clientele simply as Marie, was sitting at the counter keeping an eye on her staff, and a frown of annoyance crossed her plump face. 'Kelley, love, haven't I told you a hundred times to use the side door?'

'Sorry, Aunt Mary,' Kelley said breathlessly. 'But I just had to tell you . . . '

Marie's frown was swiftly transformed into a beaming smile and she leapt up from her chair, sweeping Kelley into a perfumed embrace. 'You've got the job then? I said you would.' Then she whispered in Kelley's ear. 'Please don't call me Mary. It's

Marie, remember?' Then she turned to her clients. 'Hear that, everyone? My niece is going to be starring in *Land Girls*.'

'Not starring,' Kelley protested. 'It's only a small part.'

'Well, you've worked hard enough for it, love.'

Marie's clients added congratulations, having watched her struggles to find work over the past few months. They'd seen her go to audition after audition only to return home disappointed.

'I told you it was only a matter of time,' said Marie.

'I couldn't have done it without Harry. I'm so lucky having such a brilliant agent.' Kelley blushed but it wasn't at the mention of Harry Levinson. Although she'd become very fond of her agent, he was old enough to be her father, not to mention being her aunt's lover.

But then Carl Roche was quite old too, and he stirred up quite different

2

feelings. She fanned herself with her script. 'It's hot in here, isn't it?' she said. 'I think I'll go up to the flat and start learning my lines. I have to be at the studio early tomorrow.'

★ ★ ★

In the flat above the salon she threw herself down on her bed and went over the exciting events of the morning. It wasn't just getting the part that had her heart racing and her brown eyes sparkling. She just couldn't believe that not only had she met and spoken to Carl Roche, but that the famous celebrity had personally chosen her out of the half-dozen young hopefuls auditioning for the popular drama series.

After more than a year working as a lowly assistant in the salon, she'd been almost ready to go back home to Sussex and get what her father called 'a proper job'. But she had made up her mind to give her longed-for acting career one more try.

A year ago she had come to London full of hope and confidence, trusting in her earlier successes in community theatre, which had earned her an Equity card. And when her aunt's agent friend, Harry Levinson, had taken her on she'd been sure that it was only a matter of time before she found work.

But months had passed and still she didn't get the break she'd been hoping for. Marie and Harry made encouraging noises before each audition, then showered her with sympathy when once more she failed to get the job.

Twice a week she phoned her father and sometimes it was an effort to stay optimistic. She knew Dad was dying to say, 'I told you so.' Her mother had always encouraged her ambitions but when she died, Dad had wanted her to stay home and work with him in the village store. She'd stayed over the busy Christmas period, but when she was ready to leave he didn't want her to go.

With each month that passed it had

been harder to get away. But finally on her nineteenth birthday she'd made the decision. 'I'm sorry, Dad. I must give it a try,' she'd pleaded, and he'd given in reluctantly.

The hoped-for acting parts hadn't materialised, but she couldn't accept defeat and go home. Her savings were fast running out, so to pay for her keep she'd been working in the salon, tidying up after the other assistants and keeping the customers supplied with drinks and magazines.

'Maybe Dad was right. Acting's OK as a hobby but perhaps I'm not meant to be a professional,' she'd confided to Marie after yet another disappointing audition.

'Don't give up hope, love. Harry's doing his best. Meantime, I can find plenty for you to do in the salon. It's good to have an extra pair of hands.'

'But I can't stay here forever. I'll wear out my welcome. And I can't afford a place of my own yet. Perhaps I should go back to Holton.'

'Give it a bit longer — say till Easter. I'm sure something will turn up.'

Kelley nodded gratefully. She didn't really want to give up yet.

A few weeks later, Marie said, 'It's about time you did something with your hair. A hairdo always cheers a woman up. It used to be a new hat, but you young things don't wear hats anymore. So come here and let me use my artistic talents on you.'

Kelley laughed and gave in gracefully. She wasn't too sure when Marie suggested lightening her long hair to a pale ash blonde, but she had to agree the effect was stunning. She looked like a different person. When Harry turned up that evening to take them for a meal, he whistled appreciatively.

'What a lucky man I am, having two beautiful women to take out,' he chuckled, escorting them down the stairs and seeing them into his car with a flourish.

Whether it was the confidence inspired by the new hairstyle or whether she was just due for a break, Kelley wasn't sure. But a few days later Harry had rung to tell her that River View Productions, an independent studio run by Carl Roche, was holding auditions. A top media personality, Roche had been a chat show host before starting his own television company. Now he made documentaries and drama series, including the very popular *Land Girls*.

Kelley had gone off to the audition full of hope, but her steps dragged as she neared the studio, anticipating yet another let-down.

★ ★ ★

River View Productions was housed in a former warehouse in London's Dockland which, until a few years ago, had stood derelict and empty. Now the area was undergoing a transformation. The old dockside buildings had been converted into luxurious apartments and offices. A few, like River View, were used as studios by the entertainment industry. Carl Roche had spared no expense in making his premises fit the image of his prestigious company.

Kelley stepped out of Wapping Underground station and turned down a narrow road. Her high heels stumbling on the stone setts which were still occasionally visible through the asphalt, she came to another street which was barred to traffic by old up-ended cannons acting as bollards. The front of the tall building was in shadow, the entrance hard to find. But once inside, she looked round in amazement.

The front lobby was full of people, all intent on their own concerns. She gave her name to the receptionist, who ticked her off on a list, beckoning another girl to show her the way to the studio. Kelley followed her through a warren of sets and editing suites until they stopped at the door to Studio Three. 'Through there,' the girl said, indicating that Kelley should just walk in.

With a dry mouth she entered, and a young man with a clipboard beckoned her over. Once more her name was ticked off. She looked round at the other young hopefuls, some of whom she recognised from earlier auditions. They exchanged nervous smiles, then turned to the director.

'It's Simon Kent,' one of the girls said in an awed whisper. Kelley recognised the name and her nervousness increased.

The director, casually dressed in jeans and a sweatshirt, ran his hands through his shaggy hair and pushed his glasses up his nose. Then he cleared his throat and called, 'Kelley Robinson? Over here, please.'

Although her only experience was with theatre work, Kelley had learned a lot from doing her demonstration DVD and from the many auditions she'd attended over the past few months. Once she started reading the part, her nerves vanished and she threw herself into it with enthusiasm.

9

When everyone had read there was a lot of hanging about until Simon, who'd been conferring with a couple of people at the back of the studio, read out two names. Kelley held her breath. ' . . . and Kelley Robinson, please,' he said. The others were dismissed.

The three remaining applicants were asked to read again. Kelley was the last, her stomach knotted with nerves. Did she really stand a chance?

'Right, girls,' Simon said, pushing his glasses up onto his forehead. 'We'll call you back in a bit. Go and get some tea.'

When they returned, Kelley was so nervous it almost didn't sink in until the other two girls turned to leave. She'd got the part.

'Oh, thank you, Mr Kent,' she said, eyes shining.

'Don't thank me, pet. Mr Roche made the final decision.' Simon waved his hand towards the back of the studio, where a tall well-built man with silvery blond hair stood quietly talking to one of the cameramen.

Kelley gasped. She hadn't expected to see the great man himself. He usually kept more to the production and business side of things these days.

She dragged her eyes away and concentrated on Simon. 'Eight o'clock sharp, tomorrow morning,' he said. Kelley smiled and nodded, impatient to get away now and tell Marie and Harry her exciting news.

As she turned to leave, Carl Roche came towards her. 'Kelley, welcome to *Land Girls*. I hope you'll enjoy being part of our team.' He took her unresisting hand, smiling down at her with his incredibly blue eyes.

'Thank you, Mr Roche,' she stammered, feeling her cheeks redden.

'Carl, not mister,' he said, still holding on to her hand. 'We're very informal on the set.' He released her hand and she rushed away.

On the tube going back to Notting Hill she went over the encounter in her mind. *How naive he must have thought me. A real country bumpkin*, she thought. But he was a celebrity and very good-looking. Perhaps her reaction wasn't so unusual. But he *was* the boss. She'd have to learn to talk to him without blushing and going weak at the knees, like a schoolgirl meeting a pop star, she told herself firmly.

Now, lying on her bed and re-living the moment she'd met Carl, she could still feel the warmth of his hand and the sense of intimacy as he spoke her name. Was she being naive in reading so much into such a brief encounter?

She was brought back to earth by a sharp knock on the door. 'I've made us some lunch, love. Come down when you're ready,' Marie called.

Kelley jumped off the bed and opened the door. She followed her aunt into the kitchen. 'Just a snack today,' Marie said. 'We're going out tonight to celebrate. Harry's booked us a table at Patti's.'

Kelley was too excited to eat but Marie urged her to try. 'Now, love, tell me all about it.'

'It's only a small part. But I think it's thanks to you I got it. They wanted a blonde you see,' said Kelley, running her hands though her hair.

'Your mum would be so proud,' Marie said wistfully.

'I still miss her so much,' Kelley said. 'She'd be thrilled to know I'm working for Carl Roche — she was such a fan of his show.'

'I didn't realise he was involved in *Land Girls*,' Marie said. 'So — what's the part?'

'The girl I'm playing is called Violet and she's going to cause havoc in the village because she pinches the other girls' boyfriends. It sounds like fun.'

'It'll be hard work too, you know. It's not all glamour,' Marie warned.

'I know that,' Kelley said, tossing her head. 'Anyway, Carl said I'm a natural. He was so nice, Marie. He said he knew I was right for the part as soon as I started to read.'

'Oh Carl, is it? When did you get so

friendly with Mr Roche?'

Kelley stiffened at her aunt's tone. 'He told me to call him Carl.'

'Well, don't get too friendly, that's all. He has a reputation, you know — especially with young blondes.' She stood up and put her arm round Kelley's shoulders. 'I wouldn't want you to get hurt.'

'Don't be silly.' Kelley shrugged her off. 'Besides, he's married.'

Marie sighed. 'It's none of my business, love. You're a grown woman able to make your own decisions. I just don't want you to make a wrong one, that's all.'

Kelley left the table, annoyed at her aunt's interfering. 'Don't worry, I'm not that stupid.' She paused at the door. 'Sorry, I didn't mean to snap. But I thought you'd be pleased for me, being singled out by such a celebrity.'

'Of course I'm pleased — that you got the part anyway. Are you going to ring your dad?'

'I don't think he'd be interested. He

doesn't think acting's a proper job anyway.'

'Of course he'll be interested. Ring him, Kelley.' Marie's tone was firm and Kelley was stricken with guilt.

When Marie had gone downstairs, Kelley settled down to read the script and learn her lines. It was only a small part but she was determined to give it her all. Carl had hinted that the part of Violet would be expanded in future episodes.

'Carl,' she whispered, picturing his warm smile and twinkling blue eyes. Instead of concentrating on the script she found herself once more re-living the encounter. A spasm of annoyance crossed her face as she thought of what her aunt had said. Why did she have to spoil things? There was always gossip about famous people — it didn't mean it was true. She shook her head and turned a page of the script. What was she doing, daydreaming about a man she'd only just met — a married man at that?

2

By the time Marie came upstairs after closing the salon, Kelley had accepted that her aunt only had her best interests at heart. But she decided not to mention Carl again. After all, she wasn't sure if he *was* interested in her. Perhaps he was just being kind.

She had poured a gin and tonic, Marie's favourite after-work drink, and she handed her aunt the glass as she kicked off her shoes and sank into a chair.

'You'd better get your glad rags on if we're going out. Harry will be here soon,' Marie said, taking a long slurp from the glass. 'Boy, I needed that. What a day.'

'Sorry I wasn't there to give you a hand,' Kelley said.

'Don't worry, love,' Marie replied with a chuckle. 'I can get a work experience kid to do the clearing up.'

'I don't expect this job will last long anyway, so I'll be back in the salon before long,' Kelley said. She didn't dare hope that the part in *Land Girls* would be permanent and she knew that actors were more often out of work than in.

Marie tried to cheer her up. 'You'll be so good they'll write you a bigger part,' she said. 'Now go on, get ready.'

Kelley had just finished her make-up when the doorbell rang. She flicked the brush through her hair and ran downstairs, throwing her arms round Harry's neck and kissing him on the cheek. 'Thank you, thank you,' she squealed.

'Only doing my job, love.' Harry disengaged himself and felt in his pocket for the ubiquitous cigar.

'Don't you light that thing in here,' Marie said, slapping at his arm.

'Come on, sweetheart, just a few puffs before we get in the taxi.' He got out his gold embossed cigarette lighter and flicked it on. 'I don't know. Where can a man smoke these days?'

'Oh, go on then, just a puff.' Marie gave in and Kelley smiled. It had taken her a while to realize that their constant bickering disguised a very deep affection.

At Patti's the maitre d' greeted them as favoured customers and led them to their usual table, pulling out their chairs and beckoning to the wine waiter.

Harry had extinguished his cigar at the door and now said, 'Well, if I can't smoke, at least I can treat us to the finest champagne.' He stood up and in a loud voice said, 'Champagne for everyone. We're celebrating.' Heads turned and there was scattered laughter. Harry Levinson was well-known for his flamboyant gestures. As the waiter filled glasses for everyone, he raised his glass. 'Here's to Kelley Robinson and her part in *Land Girls*, a rising star if ever I saw one.'

Kelley shrank in her seat as glasses were raised in a toast. A smattering of applause ran round the restaurant and Marie pulled at her arm. 'Say something, love.'

She shook her head, furious with Harry for drawing attention to her. Still, she thought, smiling shyly and nodding towards the well-wishers, if she really was going to be a star she'd have to get used to being the centre of attention.

The noise died down and the diners returned to their meals. Soon the restaurant was filled with the usual chatter, the clink of china and cutlery, and soft music playing in the background.

Grateful that she was no longer in the limelight, Kelley concentrated on her food, although from time to time she glanced round, half-hoping that Carl would turn up. This was also one of his favourite haunts.

She was trying to decide whether or not to have a sweet when she looked up, frowning when she saw Paul Ericson standing there. She'd met the journalist several times at her aunt's parties but she'd tried to avoid him. He was always popping up alongside his mate, the photographer Mick Gamble. She dreaded seeing her picture in the tabloids.

Marie had greeted him with a kiss on each cheek. 'Paul, darling, we're celebrating. Why don't you join us?' She glanced behind him. 'No Mick tonight?'

'No, he's got a photo shoot.'

'Good, then I don't have to worry about how I look.' Marie gave a little laugh.

'You always look lovely, Marie,' Paul said, pulling out a chair. 'Now, what are you celebrating?'

Kelley cringed as her aunt proceeded to sing her praises, making much more of the small part she'd landed than was warranted. 'She's a rising star,' Marie gushed.

Paul turned to her with a smile, showing even white teeth against tanned skin. His brown hair flopped over his forehead and he was wearing his usual scruffy old leather flying jacket. 'You must let me interview you some time. What about a spread in *OK* or *Hello*?' he said.

Kelley thought he was joking and tried to laugh it off. 'Wait till you see the show before you make rash suggestions like that,' she said.

He laughed and was about to reply when someone called to him across the room. He stood up and took Kelley's hand. 'I'm sure I'll be writing about you before long,' he said. 'Good luck with the show.'

Kelley felt a little uncomfortable at the thought of him writing about her. She did want to be successful, but she'd seen the stuff that had been written about show business people. Not that she had any guilty secrets. But she didn't fancy her father seeing her photo on the front page of the celebrity magazines — and running a news-agent's, how could he avoid it? Perhaps it wouldn't be all bad though. Paul seemed very nice and she couldn't imagine him writing anything nasty about her — after all, she hadn't got drunk at parties or taken drugs. What was there to write about other than her burgeoning career? And she had to admit that when Paul smiled he was quite attractive. Not as devastatingly handsome as Carl of course.

★ ★ ★

Kelley arrived early at the studio the next morning to find the cast already doing a walkthrough. No one took any notice of her and she stood by the door watching.

'Right everybody. Ten-minute break,' Simon called when he was finally satisfied. He spotted Kelley by the door and came over. 'Ah, here's our new girl,' he said, handing her a script and a photocopied call sheet. 'As you can see, the scene we're doing doesn't feature your character at all. We're doing the bit where they're talking about the new girl. We'll be doing the scene where

Violet arrives at the farm when we go up to Norfolk in a few weeks.' Simon smiled at her reassuringly. 'It's a lot to take in all at once, I know. Have you done any location shooting at all, pet?'

Kelley found her voice. 'I haven't done any filming at all, apart from the promotional DVD which I believe you've seen. I've only done stage work so far.'

'Not to worry. Just watch the others. You'll soon get the hang of it.' Simon seemed unfazed by the prospect of directing a complete novice.

'I hope I'll be OK. I must admit I'm nervous. It's all so different from anything I've done before.'

'You'll be OK, pet. That's why I asked you to come in today, so you could meet the others and watch how we do things. Later on I'll get someone to take you up to wardrobe.' Simon patted her hand and stood up. He went over to the group of actors who were standing around drinking coffee.

Kelley sat on the edge of her chair

clutching the script and trying to control the butterflies in her stomach. Simon was waving his arms about and looking in her direction as he spoke to a slim dark-haired woman in her forties. Were they talking about her? *I bet he's moaning because he's got to nursemaid a beginner*, she thought.

She recognised Erica Waddell, who played the pub landlady. She was an actress Kelley had long admired. She'd been looking forward to meeting her but she smiled apprehensively as Erica sat down next to her.

'Hallo, Kelley. So you're our new heartbreaker on *Land Girls*. Simon tells me you're new to filming, but don't worry. The first time is always the worst. Now come and meet the others before we start work again.'

The members of the cast were all open and friendly, especially Erica and Phil Brooks, who played the farmer in the series. The 'Land Girls' were all around Kelley's age and seemed easy to get on with. The only exception was

Judy Cotterill, who greeted Kelley very coolly.

'Where did Carl find you?' she sneered. Some of the girls giggled but Erica shushed them. Kelley felt herself reddening and an angry retort rose to her lips. But she didn't get the chance to say anything as Simon called for silence and everyone hurried to their places.

Kelley found a quiet corner where she could watch and learn. She would be up there tomorrow and she dreaded making a hash of things. She didn't want to let the rest of the cast down, especially after Judy's catty comment.

During the lunch break Erica and Phil took Kelley to the canteen on the next floor. As they went up in the lift Erica said, 'You'll soon find your way around, although this place is a bit of a warren. The main thing to remember is that apart from reception, all the ground floor is studio, and the next floor is hair, makeup and canteen. Above that is Carl's suite of offices. I did hear that he's having the top floor converted to an apartment for himself.'

'It's nothing like I imagined it,' Kelley said as they stepped out of the lift. 'I'm so lucky getting a break like this — thanks to my agent.'

'So you don't know Carl Roche then?' Erica asked curiously.

'I met him for the first time at the audition. What made you think I knew him — and what did Miss Cotterill mean by that remark?'

'That was just Judy being catty. Don't take any notice of her. No, it's just that our Carl has a bit of a reputation with young actresses, especially blondes. We thought you might have been hand-picked.'

Kelley felt her face flushing. 'No, I wasn't,' she said vehemently.

Erica laughed and patted Kelley's arm. 'Don't worry, I'll make sure no one makes any more catty remarks.'

By the end of the day Kelley's head was whirling with new faces and impressions but, once the cameras started rolling, her nerves disappeared. She was really looking forward to the next day, although she was now a bit apprehensive about seeing Carl Roche again. He'd been so nice to her at the audition and, naively, she hadn't thought anything of it. But Erica's remarks had put him in a different light and she found herself remembering what Marie had told her. But surely that was just studio gossip. Anyone as good-looking and successful as Carl was bound to be talked about.

In the tube going back to Marie's she tried to forget about Carl Roche and concentrate on what she'd learned that day. She'd known of course that the story wasn't filmed in the proper order. But it seemed strange that tomorrow she would be doing a scene with people she was supposed to know quite well. Then, when they went on location they would film her arriving in the village as a stranger. It was all so different to stage work.

She opened her bag and took out the

call sheet for the next day, which listed the performers and the times they were due at the studio as well as props, costumes and other equipment. Her name was highlighted in pink, as were the times for hair, makeup and wardrobe, and when she was due on set.

★ ★ ★

After a few days, Kelley felt as if she'd always been part of the team. At first she'd been overwhelmed by the huge studio and the number of people working there. Now she knew most of the crew by name and even had an inkling of what their jobs entailed. Her first few scenes had been nerve-wracking but Simon knew how to get the best out of people and she rewarded his patience by learning quickly.

At the end of her first week, he stopped her on the way out. 'You're doing great, pet. Keep up the good work,' he said.

Kelley blushed with pleasure and mumbled her thanks.

'One more thing though,' Simon said. 'Try to shut your mind to what's happening off set. And don't let Carl — or anyone else — make you nervous. As I said, pet, you're doing OK.'

The blush deepened, and Kelley couldn't wait to get away. The only time she seemed to forget her lines or her moves was when Carl was around. She had quickly learned that he was a perfectionist and intolerant of mistakes, which only increased her nervousness. She really wanted to justify his faith in hiring such an inexperienced actress, and she was always tinglingly aware whenever he came onto the set.

But Carl was also quick to praise when things went right, and Kelley was dumbfounded when he spoke to her after shooting had finished one day.

'I find it hard to believe you haven't done this before. You're so professional,' he said, smiling down at her.

She stammered her thanks, wishing

she could come up with something cool and witty in reply. Judy would have known just how to handle that, she told herself, envying the more experienced actress's poise and sophistication. But she couldn't forget her catty remarks that first day and it was hard not to be self-conscious when Carl spoke to her, especially as she found him so attractive.

'By the way, Kelley — did I see you talking to Paul Ericson the other day?' Carl asked. 'In Patti's?' He smiled but his voice was cool.

'Oh, yes. He's a friend of my aunt, Marie Winters.'

'I know Marie well — lovely lady,' he said. 'You live with her, don't you?'

'Just till I can find a place of my own,' Kelley said.

Carl nodded. 'Well, just a word of warning. You know what these reporters are like. If he tries to pump you, refer him to our publicity department.' He smiled. 'You're a rising star, Kelley. I've already made sure that you get the right sort of publicity — you don't need the likes of Paul Ericson to further your career.'

She thought it best not to mention that she'd been tempted to accept Paul's offer of a magazine interview.

3

Kelley felt like an old hand by the time they went up to Norfolk for location shooting. The cast was staying in the local pub, which only had a few rooms, so she agreed to share with Erica.

'Appropriate, don't you think?' Erica said, looking round the low-beamed room with its chintz curtains at the lattice windows. She played the pub landlady in the series and Kelley agreed with a smile. She liked Erica and they were becoming friends.

'I hate location shooting,' Erica said as they unpacked.

'I'm looking forward to it, although I must admit I'm nervous,' Kelley said.

'You wait, my dear. You have to get up at the crack of dawn so there's no traffic. Then there's the weather. If the storyline demands rain, we get a heatwave. And if it's bright sunshine we want, you can be sure we'll all get soaked before the day's out.' She laughed as she shook out a blouse, holding it critically up to the light before hanging it in the wardrobe.

Kelley sat on the edge of the bed, her own unpacking done. 'It can't be that bad, surely,' she said.

'Oh, I'm not trying to put you off. But you need to be aware that this job's not all glamour.'

'I'm not as naive as you seem to think,' Kelley protested, wishing they wouldn't all keep treating her like a child, even if she was the new girl.

Erica held up her hands, laughing. 'Don't bite my head off. I'm only trying to help.'

'Sorry. I know you mean to be kind.' Kelley went to the door. 'I'm going to get something to eat. I'm starving.'

Erica followed her downstairs, where they were joined in the restaurant by Phil Brooks and Judy Cotterill. The four of them had some outdoor scenes to do together the following morning.

Other cast members would be joining them later in the day. As they ate, Kelley studied them. Judy, dark and vibrant, dominated the conversation. She seemed oblivious of the stares and nudges of the other diners, as they recognised the famous television star. Kelley felt a warm glow at the thought of being on the inside.

There was a stir as someone entered the bar and attention switched from Judy to Carl Roche. He acknowledged the attention, then turned to the group at the table.

'Early call tomorrow, folks — and the weather forecast's good.' He leaned towards Kelley. 'Your first outdoor shoot. Not nervous, are you?' He put his hand on her shoulder. She felt a blush beginning and nodded shyly. 'Don't be. You'll be fine.' When she looked up from her plate he was gone.

Judy smiled slyly. 'The great man seems to have taken a shine to our Kelley,' she said.

'Leave her alone. Can't you see she's

embarrassed?' Erica said.

'He's just being kind. And he's right, I am nervous,' Kelley said faintly.

'You'll be OK after a good night's sleep. Come on, I need an early night too.' Erica stood up and Kelley followed her. At the door she turned and saw Judy whisper something to Phil, then they both burst out laughing. Judy glanced up and gave her a little wave. Kelley forced herself to smile back and followed Erica upstairs, wishing she had the easy confidence which seemed so natural to the others.

'Don't take any notice of Judy,' Erica said, as they prepared for bed. 'She's a trouble-maker. And she fancies Carl like mad. She knows she doesn't stand a chance but she gets quite touchy if she thinks he's taking an interest in anyone else, especially a young pretty girl like you.'

'I thought he was already married.'

Erica gave a snort of laughter. 'A little thing like a wife doesn't stop the Carls of this world. But he's not interested in Judy. As I told you before, he usually goes for blondes, so watch out.'

As she settled down to sleep Kelley couldn't stop thinking about Carl. He'd been very attentive ever since that first day at River View. But she couldn't believe what the others said about him. She'd seen pictures of him with his wife in the glossy magazines. Angela Roche was very beautiful in a cool English upper-class way. With a wife like that, why would he need to look elsewhere? she wondered naively. But she couldn't help thinking that if he was free she'd be more than willing to be his girlfriend.

Shooting started very early the next day and she had no chance to think about Carl or anything else except getting things right. Once she'd donned the corduroys and green jumper and rolled her hair into the wartime pageboy style, her nervousness vanished. With her lips outlined in glossy bright red, the transformation was complete. She really felt she was Violet, a confident and flirtatious land girl who was going to wreak havoc with the men of the village.

The weather was perfect for the harvest scenes and all the actors were on form. All too soon the location shooting was over, and a few days later the cast and crew were on their way back to London.

4

They had arrived back at River View and Kelley was looking forward to seeing Carl again. She knew he had other business interests besides his production company but it didn't stop her looking up each time the door opened, her heart skipping a beat. He always gave her that special smile and stopped to chat.

The sensible part of her told her she was acting like a star-struck teenager. Why would he be interested in her? Besides, Kelley was only contracted for the current series. The actress who'd been written out of the series was expected back after the birth of her baby. So she could soon be out of work. It wouldn't hurt to ask Harry to find out about any upcoming auditions.

She had stayed behind to go through

tomorrow's scenes, anxious to learn all she could about television filming. How would Simon interpret this scene? She knew how she'd do it. But it wouldn't do to voice her opinion. She was just a novice. Still, she thought that if she wasn't an actress she'd like to try directing.

Lost in thought, she jumped when a voice spoke behind her.

'You're working too hard, Kelley. You should learn to relax more.'

She turned round quickly. 'Oh, it's you.' Was it because it was Carl standing there, or would anyone disturbing her so suddenly have made her heart start thumping like this? Struggling to calm herself, she pointed to her script. 'I'm just going over tomorrow's scene,' she said.

'I didn't mean to startle you. I thought everyone had gone.' He took her arm and led her towards the door. 'And you should go too. I mean it, everyone has to relax sometime.'

Outside, he said, 'Can I drop you

anywhere?' He gestured to the sleek white Porsche.

Her first instinct was to refuse, but it was late and she didn't fancy the Underground at this time of night. She thanked him and gave him directions to her aunt's salon. She settled into the comfortable leather seat, revelling in the luxury. Naively, she was excited at being in a posh car with such a famous man. Her old school friends would be so envious. But the grown-up part of her was struggling with other emotions, and a powerful attraction that she knew she wouldn't be able to resist, despite her vow never to become involved with a married man.

It seemed only minutes before they pulled up outside Marie's salon. When the car stopped neither of them moved. The silence stretched between them. Kelley shifted in her seat, reaching down for the seat-belt.

Carl touched her hand and a jolt of electricity ran through her as his fingers enclosed hers. 'Don't go yet,' he said, turning in his seat to face her. 'Tell me, are you happy in our little family? That's what I call the team — my family.' He gave a self-conscious laugh.

'Yes,' she whispered.

'I must admit I wasn't too sure you could carry off the part of Violet. But you're good. In fact, I'm thinking of getting the scriptwriter to give you more to do. And you'll definitely be in the next series.'

Kelley gave a gasp of surprise and pleasure. She turned to him, eyes shining. 'Thank you, Mr Roche.'

'I told you to call me Carl. After all, we're going to be friends, aren't we?' He smiled at her and reached across to touch her hair. 'So young, so beautiful,' he murmured, leaning forward and dropping a kiss on her cheek. Before she could react he said, 'I think you'd better go in now.'

He leaned over and opened her door, making no move to get out himself. Kelley unclasped the seat belt and fumbled in her bag for her key.

'Good night, see you in the morning. Don't be late,' Carl called as he started the engine.

Kelley went slowly up the stairs, touching her cheek, which still burned with the feel of his lips. *I'm not going to fall for that charm of his,* she told herself. *Anyway, a kiss means nothing. Show-business people kiss each other all the time.*

But she was still trembling as she got ready for bed. And it was a long time before she finally fell asleep.

5

By the end of the summer they'd finished filming the last episode of the current series and Kelley was wondering where her next acting job was coming from. Although Carl had promised that she'd be in the next series, it still wasn't confirmed. But she wouldn't think about that now, she thought, as she settled down in front of Marie's large-screen television to watch the first episode she'd appeared in.

'This is even more exciting than my first part at the Festival Theatre,' she said. 'Do you remember, Marie? You and Mum were even more excited than I was.'

'How could I forget? I knew then that you'd make it, love.' She turned to Harry, who was beside her on the sofa. 'Didn't I tell you she was good?'

'Shhh, it's just starting,' Harry said.

Mentioning her mother brought a tear to Kelley's eye. If only she was here now, she'd be so proud of her. She wondered if Dad was watching right now. She'd phoned him, but he'd claimed that he was too busy with the shop to watch television.

She swallowed the lump in her throat and concentrated on the screen, thankful for her loyal friends. Marie and Harry's reaction was everything she had hoped for.

'Well, you certainly deserve a part in the next series,' Marie said, giving her a hug.

'And I'll make sure she gets it,' Harry said.

'Well, Carl did promise,' Kelley said.

Marie's lips tightened at the mention of Carl and she wished she hadn't spoken. Knowing how much her aunt disapproved of her admiration for the producer, she tried to avoid talking about him.

But she couldn't help falling in love. She'd had boyfriends before, but none of them had ever aroused such strong feelings in her. Just to think of Carl or hear his name mentioned brought the butterflies fluttering into her stomach, and whenever he came into a room she felt herself blushing. She tried to tell herself it was infatuation. But instead of wearing off as she got to know him better, her feelings grew stronger.

When he smiled at her, her legs began to tremble and she was sure he could hear the fierce thumping of her heart. Although he often singled her out for a word of praise at work, and sometimes gave her a lift home, he'd never given the slightest indication that he was romantically interested in her. In fact he was unfailingly polite and professional. Marie must be wrong about him, she thought. She'd never seen him chatting up the other women in the show, not even Judy, who threw herself at him whenever he appeared.

Her mobile beeped and she grabbed it off the side table. Perhaps Dad was ringing to congratulate her. But she knew it wouldn't be him. On the rare occasions he rang he used Marie's landline.

When she heard whose voice it was, thoughts of her father fled and she had to take a deep breath. 'Yes, we were watching. Thank you.'

She paused and Marie looked up at her. 'Your dad?' she mouthed.

Kelley shook her head. 'Just someone congratulating me,' she said, not wanting to tell Marie who it was. Fortunately her aunt had got up to pour a drink for Harry and didn't seem to notice her flushed face.

'Yes, all right, I'll be there,' she said, switching off the phone and turning to Marie. 'That was Erica. They're all meeting up for a drink. I said I'd join them,' she said.

She hated to lie but if she said it was Carl, she'd be subjected to another lecture. Besides, although Carl had rung her, the rest of the cast would be there too. What was wrong with having a drink with friends?

When the taxi pulled up outside the studio, she hesitated. She hadn't seen Carl since shooting had finished and she'd been missing him, longing to see him, while at the same time telling herself she was behaving like a star-struck teenager. The sound of his voice on the phone had re-awakened her feelings and she'd agreed to come just for the chance to be near him. But could she bear to spend the rest of the evening watching Judy fawning over him, seeing him laughing and flirting with the other girls in the cast?

She pushed the door open and walked into the lobby. She'd just have a quick drink and say hello to everybody. She didn't have to stay long.

As she started towards the studio where she assumed everyone would be, she realised how quiet it was. Her footsteps echoed on the tiled floor and she began to feel nervous, jumping when the door swung open. A figure was silhouetted in the doorway and she gasped when she realised who it was.

'Where is everybody?' Her heart was thumping and her voice came out in a squeak. She never knew what to say when they were alone.

'There's no one else here — it's just you and me,' he said in that soft seductive voice.

'Are we meeting them somewhere else?'

He gave a low chuckle. 'Oh, Kelley — such an innocent. Didn't you realise — I wanted to see you alone? How can I tell you how I feel when there's always hordes of people around?'

Was he saying what she thought — hoped — he was saying? Kelley smiled up at him. 'I feel the same, Carl,' she whispered.

Instead of taking her in his arms as she'd anticipated, he took her hand. 'Come with me. I've got something to show you.' He led her towards the lift and pressed the button. 'I want you to be the first to see the penthouse,' he said.

The lift stopped with a jerk and the

doors slid open. They stepped out into a corridor at the end of which was a wrought-iron spiral staircase. He gestured upwards and Kelley followed him, still in a daze. He put his key in the door at the top of the stairs and led her inside.

Her first impression was of space and light. Carl switched on lamps to reveal bare brick walls and a polished light oak floor. The cast-iron pillars of the former warehouse had been painted white. Windows took up the whole of the wall facing the river, now obscured by white blinds. The only colour came from an abstract painting taking up most of one wall — a riot of black, yellow and red, and on a small table a black onyx vase containing a spray of silk poppies.

Carl turned to her with a proud smile. 'Do you like it?' he asked.

After the Victorian-style opulence of Marie's flat and the cramped clutter of her home in Sussex, the light and space were overwhelming. 'It's like something out of a film,' she said.

Carl's warm smile told her she'd said the right thing.

'I always dreamed of having a place like this,' he said. 'I only moved in a few weeks ago. You're my first guest.' He pressed a switch on the wall. From concealed speakers the soft strains of Vivaldi streamed into the room. Smiling at her expression, he picked up the bottle of champagne which had been cooling in an ice bucket, popped the cork and poured two glasses.

Kelley had wandered over to the window and looked down at the Thames far below. She smiled at the thought that beneath his macho image, the rich and powerful Carl Roche was like a small boy trying to impress. Well, she was impressed.

As he came towards her with the glasses she turned to him, her brown eyes serious. 'Why me?' she asked. 'Why isn't your wife here?' She wished she hadn't spoken as his smile disappeared and a spasm of anger crossed his face.

But it wasn't directed at her. His eyes

grew shadowed and his voice was sombre. 'Because she doesn't want to be here. She's too busy with her horses and garden parties, she says. Too busy to share what should be the proudest moment of my life.' He waved his hand, encompassing the room, and took a sip of his champagne. 'She's just not interested. This is the symbol of my success, of all I've achieved over the years. I was like you once, Kelley — naive, unsophisticated. I started from nothing, and look at me now.' A note of pride entered his voice.

Kelley gazed up at him, love shining from her eyes. He'd seemed so self-assured, even arrogant at times, but he was vulnerable too. She wanted to comfort him. She put her glass down on the small table and reached out to touch his hand. He pulled her towards him. She knew what was going to happen and Marie's warnings flitted through her mind, only to disappear as his lips touched hers.

This time it was a proper kiss, deep

and long. With it all Kelley's reservations about him being married melted away. He needed her. Still locked together, they moved towards the futon.

★   ★   ★

Later he got up to fetch another champagne bottle and she watched him walk across the room, admiring his taut tanned body, so lean and fit. She stretched lazily, like a contented cat, and turned towards the window. The sun had gone, leaving a golden glow on the horizon which softened the stark whiteness of the room. Kelley thought it was the perfect setting for her first real experience of love.

They drank champagne and made love until the sunset had gone and shadows crept into the room. They dozed, waking to find darkness had fallen.

Carl sat up, switched on one of the lamps and reached for his watch. 'Time I got you home,' he said.

'I'd rather stay here,' Kelley murmured, running her fingers down his spine.

Carl turned to her, laughing. 'You witch. And I thought you were so shy and innocent. That's why I didn't tell you how I felt straight away. But I fell for you the first time I saw you.'

Kelley blushed. 'I felt the same way. But you were already married and I thought . . . ' She broke off, embarrassed. 'You do really love me, Carl? It's not just this?' She gestured to the bed.

Carl's head was bent as he fumbled on the floor for his clothes. 'Of course it's not. When I'm away from you I can't think of anything or anyone else.'

Kelley leaned over and kissed him. 'Where's the bathroom?' she asked.

After her shower, she wrapped herself in a fluffy towel and joined Carl, who was now fully dressed and standing by the window, keys in hand.

Kelley tried to insist on staying but he was firm. 'I'm thinking of your reputation,' he said.

53

In the car she leaned back in her seat with her hand on Carl's knee. When the Porsche purred to a stop she stretched and opened her eyes. The gold lettering over Marie's salon glinted in the light of a street lamp.

'I wish I could have stayed,' she said.

'Me too. But what about in the morning when the technicians and cast arrive at the studio?' Carl's voice had hardened.

Kelley bit her lip but she knew he was only thinking of her. She got out and leaned towards him. 'I understand. But we will be together soon, won't we,' she whispered.

Their lips met and, as his arms tightened around her, she knew he didn't really want her to go.

She went inside and leaned against the door, listening until the Porsche had pulled away. Then she flew up the stairs on light feet, only coming down to earth at the door of her bedroom. Marie's large figure was outlined against the light streaming from the room across the landing.

'You're late, love. I was starting to get worried.' Her voice was mild but Kelley sensed disapproval.

'I'm sorry, Auntie. You know what these studio parties are like.' The lie slipped out unconsciously. She wasn't ready to confide in Marie yet.

'Carl brought you home, didn't he? I saw his car out of the window.'

'Yes. What's wrong with that? It's not the first time he's given me a lift.'

'Well, you're old enough to know what you're doing. But don't say I didn't warn you.' Marie turned and shut her bedroom door, not even saying good night.

Kelley bit her lip. Carl was in love with her — that was all that mattered. The other girls in his life hadn't meant anything — he'd told her so. But somehow, with Marie's disapproving looks, the magic had gone out of the evening.

6

Kelley woke early and dressed hurriedly, anxious not to miss Carl's phone call. They hadn't made plans for the weekend but she was sure he'd ring and arrange to meet. She flushed at the memory of last night and was sure Marie could tell what had happened, although she'd accepted her apology for not ringing.

Kelley was sorry she'd upset her aunt but she didn't feel she had to account for her every movement. She might be young and inexperienced, but she was an adult and free to make her own decisions.

The phone rang and she jumped guiltily, almost tipping her chair over in her haste to answer, but Marie got there first.

'Harry and I are going out for lunch,' she said, putting the phone down. 'Do you want to join us?'

'No thanks.' She glanced towards the phone. 'I might join the cast for a drink later. Erica said she'd ring and let me know where to meet.'

'Look, I'm not checking up on you. This is your home and you're free to come and go as you please. It's just that you don't usually stay out so late and I was worried. I know you're a sensible girl and won't do anything silly.'

Kelley gave her a hug, but she didn't confide in her. Marie just wouldn't understand.

The flat was quiet when she and Harry had gone and Kelley decided to try learning her lines. But she couldn't concentrate. She picked up a magazine, then flicked the television on and off. The day stretched on in silence, broken only by the hum of the central heating boiler.

By late afternoon she realised Carl wasn't going to ring. Why hadn't they made a proper arrangement the night before? Because he didn't want to, she told herself. It had just been a one-night stand. So much for her romantic daydreams. Shame burned through her. Marie had been right all along.

★　★　★

It was late on Sunday evening when the phone rang. Marie and Harry had gone out again but Kelley had stayed behind. She hadn't been out of the flat all weekend in case Carl rang. Now she hesitated. If it wasn't him she'd be devastated but if it was, what would she do? She stared at the phone for a few seconds before leaping up and grabbing it. It was him.

'Kelley, darling, how can you forgive me?'

She melted at the tender words, her anger vanishing at the sound of his voice. 'What is there to forgive?' she asked.

'I should have phoned. I meant to. But — oh God, it's been such a dreadful weekend.'

'What's happened? Are you all right?'

'I'm fine — especially now I've heard your voice. Kelley, I must see you.'

'You can't come here.'

'Come to River View then. Get a taxi.'

Her hands trembling, she grabbed her coat and bag and raced downstairs. At the end of the street she paused. She should have phoned for a taxi. There weren't many about this late on a Sunday but, as she hesitated, a cab slowed at the junction. She jumped in, gabbling the address.

He was waiting at the entrance to the studio. In the lift he clung to her. 'God I've missed you so,' he said.

She returned his kisses hungrily. Inside the flat, they fell onto the futon and satisfied their need for each other. Later Carl groaned and turned away from her, his arm flung across his face. The vast room was shadowy, lit only by stray bars of light from buildings across the river. Kelley switched a lamp on and looked down at him.

'What's wrong, darling? Tell me, please.'

He turned to her, pain in his eyes. 'It's Angela — my wife. I went down to see her, to ask her . . . ' He groaned again. 'Oh God, she's such a cold bitch.' He sat up and reached out to Kelley. 'She won't give me a divorce. I told her I loved you but she wouldn't listen. It's not as if she cares about me; she's never been a proper wife.' He buried his face in Kelley's shoulder.

She patted his back and murmured, 'It doesn't matter. I'm here. I care.' She was filled with love for him. He needed her. She would make him happy, she thought as she drifted off to sleep.

When she woke it was light and, gasping, she reached for her watch. It was seven o'clock, time to start work. So much for Carl protecting her reputation, she thought, picturing the smirks on the faces of her colleagues in the studio below. But she didn't care.

They went down in the lift together

but Carl stopped off at his office, leaving her to go on down to the studio alone. 'See you later?' she said hopefully. But he was gone without a backward glance.

7

'Carl, how much longer must we hide?' Kelley asked timidly. So far she'd obeyed his rules. But they'd been lovers for nearly three months now and she was finding it harder to pretend. She hated lying to Marie, although she suspected her aunt knew what was going on. True to her promise she hadn't interfered, although she didn't hide her disapproval when Kelley came home just for a change of clothing. The silences between them spoke more than words.

Harry had tried remonstrating with her. 'You're upsetting Marie. She promised your father she'd look out for you. Besides, she's worried about you.'

'It's none of your business. I'm not a child,' she snapped. Harry had let the matter drop but Kelley was sorry she'd hurt them.

Christmas had been hard without Carl. He'd gone down to Lydford — Angela had been taken ill, he said, begging her to understand. He couldn't possibly leave her alone over the holiday. Kelley, loving him for caring about his cold, unloving wife, had let him go without recrimination.

Unable to cope with the strained atmosphere at Marie's, she went down to Holton to visit her father. Things weren't much better there. Although proud of his daughter's success in *Land Girls*, he questioned her decision to live in London.

'Lots of people commute from here. Why don't you?' he'd asked.

'It's not nine to five, Dad. I'd have to leave here at four in the morning most days. Surely you don't expect me to do that.'

He gave a sheepish smile. 'It was just an idea, love. I miss you.'

'I'm sorry, Dad. But I'm doing so well now. You knew this was what I always wanted.' Kelley dropped a kiss on his head and promised to try and get home more often.

When she returned to London the atmosphere at Marie's was still strained. It was no good. She'd have to find a place of her own. But she hung on, hoping that Carl would ask her to move in with him.

A few weeks after Christmas, when shooting of the new series of *Land Girls* was underway, she approached the subject cautiously. 'I can't stay at Marie's much longer. I'm sure she knows, or suspects, about you.'

'I've explained over and over, Kelley. I can't let Angela down in spite of everything.'

'But you said . . . '

'I know what I said. And it's true. It's over between us. But since her illness . . . ' He shrugged helplessly. 'The doctor said she mustn't be upset. And if she found out you'd moved in with me . . . '

'I understand, darling. You're too good for her. It's just that I want us to be together.'

'So do I, darling.' Carl leaned over, stroking her hair and tracing the outline of her cheek. 'I hate it when you have to leave.' He kissed her, pulling her towards him. Kelley responded, drowning in his embrace.

Once they started making love all rational thought fled. She believed everything he told her because she wanted to. She knew his reputation but she told herself this was different. He really loved her.

Recently, however, she'd discovered his dark side, although there was always a reason for him losing his temper. He was a perfectionist and he often shouted at the cast and crew on the set. With her, though, he was always gentle and considerate. She refused to believe the rumours of his ruthlessness, the broken hearts and careers left in his wake.

He was successful. And all successful men had enemies, she told herself, stifling any unwelcome doubts that dared to surface.

Carl sat at his desk brooding, indecisive for the first time in his life. It was Kelley's fault. What was it about the girl that had him risking everything he'd worked for? He swore and swept a pile of papers to the floor. He'd have to give her up. It would be hard, but Angela had given an ultimatum. 'One more blonde bimbo and we're finished. Next time I see your name spread across the gossip columns, it's the end.'

He'd been lucky so far. But Paul Ericson and his photographer friend were always hanging out with Harry Levinson. It wouldn't be long before his relationship with Kelley was all over the tabloids.

He picked up the script for the next episode of *Land Girls*. Kelley's character had been given more prominence — at his own instigation, he admitted. 'I should have killed her off,' he muttered, slashing the page with a red pen. But Violet had proved immensely popular with the viewers and he couldn't jeopardise the success of the series. Besides, he couldn't give her up — not yet anyway.

He groaned and sunk his head in his hands. 'She's just another girl,' he muttered through clenched teeth. But she wasn't. Kelley was special. He wanted to be with her all the time, but he couldn't let her move into the penthouse.

He thought for a moment and pressed the intercom button. 'Miss Clegg, see if Kelley Robinson is still in the building and send her up. I need to discuss these scripts with her,' he said.

Kelley came in, breathless from running up the stairs. 'The lift's full up. Everyone's going home. You just caught me.'

'I won't keep you long, Miss Robinson,' Carl said formally. The secretary hovered in the doorway. 'You may go now, Miss Clegg.'

As the outer door slammed, Carl took her in his arms, stroking her face.

'I've found a flat for you,' he said.

Kelley's face fell but he kissed her, stifling her protests. 'I know you want to move in with me but . . . ' He took her hand. 'Come with me,' he said. At the end of the corridor he opened a door and took a key from his pocket. 'Your new home,' he said.

It was small, just one room with a kitchen area and a small bathroom. But it was beautifully decorated and fitted out. 'I can't afford this,' she said.

'You don't have to. It's yours.'

'But what will people think? Everyone knows you own the building.'

'As far as they're concerned you'll be paying rent. Kelley, don't you understand? Just leave some of your things lying around and invite Erica or Judy up occasionally so they think you're living here. Your real new home is on the top floor.' He pointed to the wrought-iron stairs which led up to the penthouse.

Kelley turned to him, tears trembling on her lashes. 'You really want me to move in with you? Oh Carl, I'm so happy.' She threw her arms round him.

'No one must know, not even Marie — especially Marie. Promise me now. Angela mustn't find out.' His eyes clouded. 'I feel so guilty already, carrying on like this when she's so ill.' As he held her close and stroked her hair, he grinned over her shoulder. Really, he was such a good actor. Maybe he should give himself a part in one of his own shows.

*　*　*

When she got back to Marie's, the place was heaving. Harry had landed a Hollywood contract for one of his clients and, as usual, had thrown an impromptu party. Marie spotted Kelley in the hall and beckoned her in, waving her champagne glass and smiling broadly. 'Paul's here. He's been asking after you.'

'I don't want to talk to him,' Kelley protested.

But Marie was persistent, catching her arm to hold her attention. 'He wants to write about you,' she said.

'I can't talk to him.' Kelley was terrified of revealing her affair to the journalist.

'Why can't you be nice to him? He only wants to have a chat.' She grabbed Kelley's arm and turned her to face the reporter.

'It's OK. You don't have to,' Paul said, smiling. 'We journalists aren't always popular. Besides, I'm off duty now that I've spoken to Harry's client.'

'I thought journalists were never off duty.' Carl's paranoia about the press had rubbed off on her.

Paul smiled sympathetically. 'I'll admit I'm always on the lookout for a story. It's my living, after all. But I've done my stint for tonight. Why don't we have a chat? I promise I won't write a word without your permission.'

Kelley gave in and followed him into the other room. They sat down and appraised each other. She couldn't help comparing Paul's jeans and battered leather jacket with Carl's expensively casual look.

But as they chatted, Kelley found herself warming to Paul. He didn't try to trap her into making revelations about her employer and she gradually relaxed and started to enjoy herself.

Paul was an intelligent and amusing companion. Since her involvement with Carl she'd had very little social life. Occasionally they'd go out for a meal, but he was paranoid about the press and chose quiet little pubs across the river. They were only ever seen together with people from the studio. Their contact in public was stilted and formal. Carl was jealous, too, and often Kelley had felt uncomfortable when talking to other men, knowing his eyes were on her. It was good to be able to relax and enjoy an innocent friendship without having to explain herself.

By the end of the evening she felt she'd known Paul forever. The other guests were leaving and Marie came over to them.

'You two seem to have been having a good time.' Her voice was warm with approval and Kelley knew Marie was pleased that she'd hit it off with the journalist. Her aunt had often introduced her to young men, hoping she'd grow out of her infatuation with Carl. But it was no use. Nice as Paul was, he could never measure up to her lover. Nevertheless, she had to admit she'd enjoyed the evening.

As he said goodbye, Kelley said, 'I will give you an interview — but on my terms. Set it up with Harry.'

Afterwards she regretted the impulse, wondering what Carl would say. He liked to control the publicity for himself and his television shows. It was too late now, and anyway it was nothing to do with him if Paul wanted to talk about her work. Her growing number of fans would enjoy reading about her rise to fame, but she'd be careful not to mention Carl.

When everyone had gone she helped Marie to clear up the mess left by the party. She still hadn't told her aunt she was moving out. It could wait till tomorrow. But as she turned towards the door, Marie said, 'You wanted to talk to me, love? We don't seem to have had much to say to each other lately, but if you're not too tired . . . '

'I know you've my best interests at heart,' Kelley said, 'and you promised Dad you'd look out for me. But I need my own space,' Kelley said. 'It's best if I move out . . . '

'You're not moving in with Roche,' Marie interrupted. 'How could you? Why won't you listen?' She stood up. 'Well, don't come crying to me when it all goes wrong.'

Kelley bit her lip. She'd been prepared for this, but she was still upset. 'I've told you there's nothing between Carl and me. He's my boss and he's a married man.' She felt her face grow hot at the lie.

Marie wasn't convinced. 'I know

you're all starry-eyed about him. But I know him. He never passes up an opportunity to bed a willing female, especially one as young and pretty as you.' She put a hand on Kelley's arm. 'Can't you see, love? He's just using you.'

'You're jumping to conclusions, Auntie. As it happens I'm not moving in with him. I'm renting a flat in the River View building.' Kelley hated lying, but she consoled herself that it was partly true. When Carl had sorted things out with Angela and they could publicly be together, she was sure Marie would be happy for her.

'Who else lives there?' Marie asked suspiciously.

'I don't know. People who work at the studio, I suppose. The flats have only just been finished.'

'Well, I can't stop you. But I don't know what your father's going to say.'

Kelley went to bed but lay awake half the night, consumed with guilt at hurting and deceiving the woman who'd been like a mother to her.

In the morning she packed her things and rang for a taxi to take her to River View. Marie stayed in her room and didn't come out to say goodbye.

8

Over the next few weeks Kelley gradually moved more of her belongings into the penthouse and spent little time in her studio flat. Even when Carl was away, which was often, she preferred to sleep there, surrounded by his possessions.

Despite her obsession with him, she managed to maintain her professionalism at work, surprising herself with her ability to seem cool and indifferent when Carl was on set. She was discovering just how good an actress she was.

The present series of *Land Girls* was almost completed and it was uncertain whether there would be another. Carl had promised that she wouldn't be out of work for long but she was beginning to wonder if his promises meant anything. He was still insisting on secrecy, but how long would it be before they were caught on camera by the paparazzi?

He was away again — on business, he said, but Kelley had a sneaking suspicion he'd gone to see Angela. As she wandered around the apartment, touching Carl's things and missing him dreadfully, she tried to tell herself that she understood. His wife was ill and he didn't want to upset her by mentioning divorce again. But it had gone on too long.

Suddenly the future seemed very uncertain and Kelley bit back a sob. Was she just another in Carl's long line of conquests? If only he was here, he'd reassure her — and, of course, she would believe every word.

Am I so weak? she asked herself. She did love Carl, but he wasn't her whole life. She had her career — that was, if Harry had found her some work. She hadn't seen or spoken to him or Marie since she'd moved in with Carl and she was unhappy about the rift between them. Afraid of being rejected, she'd been reluctant to make the first move. But she couldn't put it off any longer.

When she arrived at Harry's office, their conversation was stilted at first, concentrating on business matters. But when Kelley asked how Marie was, he leaned forward and pointed a finger at Kelley. 'She's still very upset. Why haven't you at least phoned, or asked her round to see your new place?'

'I thought she'd washed her hands of me.'

'You know she didn't mean it. We're both very fond of you and Marie worries about you. Goddamit, girl, at least give her a ring.'

'I didn't mean to hurt her. But she was carrying on like she was my mother. And I was sick of being treated like a baby. I didn't fall in love with Carl just to annoy her, you know.' Kelley stopped and put her hand over her mouth. After all these months of denying their affair, she'd really let the cat out of the bag now.

Harry nodded, leaning back in his chair. His eyes gleamed behind the glasses. 'So there is something between you. Oh, you silly girl.' He sounded more sad than accusing.

'It's not like you think. We love each other. When his divorce comes through we're going to get married.'

Harry gave a disbelieving snort. 'Don't tell me you fell for that one.'

'Oh, it's no use talking to you. You're just like everybody else.'

'Hang on there, girl. It's nothing to do with me, but I don't like to see Marie upset. Rightly or wrongly, she regards you as her responsibility. Most of all, she doesn't want you to be unhappy. But I can see the Cockroach has you well and truly hooked. Nothing I say will make any difference.' He reached for a cigar.

'Don't call him that,' Kelley protested.

'Sorry, love. As I say, it's nothing to do with me. Just one thing — if he lets you down, if you're ever in any trouble at all, just come to me or Marie. We'll be here for you. Now, let's drop the subject.'

Kelley was on the verge of tears. While she tried to compose herself Harry fiddled with the papers on his desk. He'd managed to find Kelley a part in a commercial to fill in the break in filming *Land Girls*.

'It's only a few days' work at most but it's better than nothing. We'll have to look around for something else soon. I've got a feeling that if another series of *Land Girls* does come off, it'll be the last. Carl likes to finish while the show's still at the top rather than doing it to death.'

'I agree, Harry. It's just about played out. But I've had an idea about that.'

'Oh, what's that then?'

'A follow-up series about what happens to them all after the war.'

'Sounds good. Why don't you write an outline, set out your ideas, and talk to Carl about it? I don't like the man but he's got a good business head. He'll tell you if it's workable.'

Kelley left Harry's office feeling much happier. He'd promised to keep quiet about Carl and she'd promised to phone Marie and try to clear the air between them. She was glad she could stop lying now — at least to them.

As she strode down the Strand and into Trafalgar Square, heads turned and several people nudged and whispered, recognising the rising television star. But she was oblivious to the stares, her head full of plans for the future.

Although she still enjoyed acting, she'd become interested in the technical side of film making and dreamed of trying her hand at directing or producing. After all, many successful directors like Carl who now had their own production companies had started out on the other side of the camera. Now her head buzzed with ideas for a new series and she couldn't wait to get home and start writing. She longed to share her ideas with Carl and wondered when he'd be back.

Back at River View, she went straight up to the top floor. She made a cup of coffee and walked through to Carl's study. For several minutes she stood looking at the computer screen, debating whether to switch it on. This was one room she'd hardly been in and she had a feeling Carl wouldn't be too happy if he caught her using his computer. But she'd done a course at college and she knew how to use it.

She switched it on and found the word processing screen. When she started typing, her fingers flew over the keys, trying to keep up with the ideas which flowed quickly one after the other. She had no idea how to set out a script so she just wrote it as a story. When she'd finished, she switched on the printer, saved the programme and printed the pages. Taking a pen out of the desk drawer, she went through to the living room, ignoring the mug of cold coffee standing on the desk.

Sitting in an armchair facing the window she read the story, crossing out and making amendments as new ideas occurred to her. After an hour she stood up, stretching and flexing her cramped fingers, but well satisfied with her work.

She went into the kitchen, suddenly realising she was hungry. While she waited for the kettle to boil she opened the fridge and took out cheese and salad to make a sandwich. Back in her armchair, she continued to make notes. The afternoon passed quickly as she sat among the remnants of her lunch, scribbling frantically. She'd type it all up again later, after she'd spoken to Carl.

The sound of his key in the door startled her and she jumped up hastily to greet him, glancing guiltily at her watch. Usually she'd have changed before he got back. He appreciated her efforts to look good for him. But it was too late now.

'I can't wait to show you what I've been doing,' she said, reaching up for his kiss. He didn't reply and she realised how tired he looked. She stroked his back, kissing him again and pressing her body against his. 'I've missed you, darling,' she whispered.

Instead of responding as he usually did, he pushed her away, looking round the big room with a frown.

'What on earth's been going on in here? Just look at the state of the place. God, you're such a slut,' he spat.

Kelley recoiled in shock. 'What's wrong?' she said looking round the room.

'Look at this mess.' He picked up the dirty crockery, crashing it into the sink. He screwed her notes up and threw them after it, then marched into the study.

Kelley leaned against the wall, numb with shock. Why was he behaving like this? What had she done? She drew a shaky breath and followed him into the other room.

'Carl, what's the matter? Is it Angela?' What else could have upset him like this?

He turned towards her, his eyes chips of ice. 'I'm only gone for a few days and look what you get up to. I don't recall giving you permission to use my computer.' He picked up the mug she'd left there, throwing it across the room. Kelley watched in mute horror as brown rivulets ran down the pristine white wall. 'I don't want you in here, looking through my papers, messing about with my things.'

Before she could draw breath to protest he came towards her, forefinger extended, stepping close to her and shouting in her face. 'And why don't you learn to clear up after yourself? I won't have my home turned into a pig sty.'

Inwardly trembling but refusing to be intimidated, Kelley found her voice. 'Hardly a pig sty, Carl. I just made myself a sandwich, that's all. And I haven't had time to clear away.'

His eyes narrowed and his hand came up. Kelley couldn't stop herself flinching. But his hand dropped to his side and he went out, slamming the door.

Stifling her tears, she went into the kitchen and rescued her notes from the kitchen sink. The papers were soaked but she folded them together and tucked them into her bag. Then she set about cleaning up the broken china and washing the floor and walls of the study. As she worked she shook with anger. How dare he talk to her like that? What had she done wrong?

She should walk out; refuse to allow herself to be treated like that. But he hadn't actually hit her. Gradually she stopped trembling, trying to work out why he'd been so angry. She knew everything in the apartment had to be just so. He'd once confessed that his fanatical tidiness was a revulsion against the squalor of his upbringing and, as she scrubbed and cleaned, she tried desperately to understand.

The physical action of cleaning calmed her down, and when she'd finished she sat by the window watching the lights of London winking on through the gathering dusk. It was a view which never palled, and helped to soothe her shattered nerves.

She didn't turn round when Carl returned but kept her eyes on the window, watching his reflection warily in the glass. He put his hands on her shoulders and bent to kiss her neck. When she didn't respond he sank to his knees beside the chair, putting his arms round her and drawing her towards him. Neither of them said a word.

A sound like a stifled sob escaped him and he clutched her more tightly. She put her hand up and, as if she were comforting a child, patted his back, as he muttered incoherent words against her shoulder.

After a long time, he released her and sat back, looking into her eyes. 'God, Kelley. How could I hurt you like that? I don't know what came over me.'

Kelley bit her lip and put out a hand to touch his face. 'I didn't mean to make you angry,' she whispered. At the same time a little voice inside asked why she was the one apologising.

'Let's not say any more about it,' he said, pulling her to him and kissing her hungrily. 'I've missed you so,' he murmured. Almost against her will, she found herself responding to him as she always did. He could make her forget everything in the passion of the moment.

Later, as he slept beside her, she looked down at him, hardly able to believe this was the same man. Had she imagined the violence in his eyes as he shouted and raved at her? And all over a few dirty dishes. She stifled the niggle of apprehension in her head. It was just a squabble, nothing serious. All couples quarrelled. And she had to admit she'd enjoyed the making up. If anything, Carl had been more passionate than ever.

*   *   *

Kelley had arranged the interview with Paul Ericson for the next day. He was coming to her flat with Mick Gamble, the photographer. She still hadn't told Carl about it, but after his behaviour last night she was reluctant to risk him losing his temper again.

She was relieved when he told her he had a business meeting, and as soon as he'd left she went down to the studio flat. She whisked round with a duster and plumped up cushions, hiding books and papers behind the sofa, reflecting wryly that Carl had a point. She *was* untidy. But hardly a slut, she thought. It looked presentable enough.

She'd just finished when the doorbell rang. She offered her visitors coffee and settled on the sofa. Paul switched on his tape recorder while Mick prowled the room, playing with the lights and twitching the curtains as he decided where to take his pictures.

As she and Paul chatted, Kelley managed to ignore the photographer and concentrate on the interview. Paul was good at his job and she found herself opening up to him as she had at

Marie's party. It was almost like a chat between friends.

She told him about her childhood in Holton, her mother's ambitions for her and her sorrow that she hadn't lived to see her burgeoning success. It wasn't until Paul touched on more recent events that she became wary.

'I heard you'd fallen out with Marie.'

'Not true. I needed my own space, that's all.' Her voice was steady but she felt her face growing hot. But it was true, she thought. They hadn't exactly quarrelled. And she'd since spoken to her aunt on the phone.

'Did your moving out have anything to do with Carl Roche?' Paul asked.

'What makes you think that?'

Paul glanced across at Mick, who raised his eyebrows. Kelley realised she'd been too vehement. She tried to regain control.

'Look Paul, I agreed to talk to you about my early life and how I got my first break. That's what you said you wanted to write about. As far as I'm concerned I've given you all the information you need.'

She stood up, reached over and switched off the tape recorder. 'The interview's over. I think you'd better go now.'

Paul put his notebook in his pocket, picked up the tape recorder and moved towards the door.

'Hey, I haven't got the pictures yet,' Mick protested.

'You'll have to use some from my file. See Harry about it.' Kelley opened the door and stood to one side.

Muttering, Mick stepped out into the corridor. Paul followed but turned back and said, 'Carl Roche owns this building, doesn't he?'

Kelley didn't answer. Tight-lipped, she closed the door. The interview hadn't gone as she'd planned. She'd seen in their eyes what they thought. Her haste to get rid of them had only confirmed their suspicions and she dreaded Carl's reaction when the article was published. She could only hope Paul would keep his word and just write what they'd agreed on. Somehow she doubted it. And it wasn't only Carl's reaction that worried her. Her father would hate it. But Carl was the one she was worried about.

'I'd best tell him and get it over with,' she said aloud. But at the top of the stairs she paused, remembering that he wasn't there. From below came the hum of voices and machinery. Although work on *Land Girls* had finished for a while, there were projects still going on. The studios and offices were a hive of activity. But up here she felt cut off from everything.

She'd have to get more work to keep her occupied. It wouldn't matter so much if Carl could spend more time with her.

She sighed and went back to her flat, retrieving the coffee-stained sheets of paper from her bag. She carried them over to the table under the window, smoothing them out and trying to read the blurred writing. *I really must get myself a laptop*, she thought, copying the notes onto a fresh page of her notebook. As she wrote, she pictured herself working with Carl. Would he like her ideas? In her excitement at the thought of being in on the creation of a brand-new series, she almost forgot her apprehension about his reaction to the interview.

9

Kelley glanced round the penthouse, making sure nothing was out of place. The cleaner had been in that morning and all the surfaces gleamed. The cushions looked as if no one had ever sat in the chairs and the glass and chrome sparkled in the late evening sun. Carl would have nothing to complain about tonight.

She had prepared the meal earlier and now she laid the table, placing tall red candles in the centre surrounded by wreaths of carnations. She stepped back to gauge the effect and smiled. This dinner must be perfect.

Satisfied that everything was ready, she changed into the new dress she'd bought a few days ago, a slim-fitting wisp of white filmy material with a splash of red poppies down the front. She brushed her hair and refreshed her lipstick, smiling as she heard Carl's key in the lock.

He came in and stopped short, waving his hand at the decorated table and the opened bottle of wine. 'What are we celebrating?' he asked.

Kelley smiled up at him and led him towards the table. 'Nothing really. I just wanted to show you how much I love you.'

He took her in his arms and the tension of a few days earlier was swept away. Breathlessly she pulled away and picked up the bottle. She poured wine for both of them and they toasted each other with their eyes across the table. She leaned towards him, smiling. Everything was just perfect. He smiled back, a look full of love. As the meal progressed, she relaxed, sure now that there would be no repeat of the violence that had so frightened her. In fact, she could almost imagine that it had never happened.

Carl pushed his plate away, leaned forward and took her hand. 'That was wonderful, darling. You certainly know how to look after a man.' There was something in his expression that said he wasn't just referring to the meal. She felt a little frisson of anticipation. Their lovemaking tonight would be really special.

But it was early yet. She wanted to talk to him first, while he was in a mellow mood. They took their wine into the living room and relaxed on the futon. Snuggled there in his arms, Kelley felt the moment was right to tell him about her project.

'I've had a marvellous idea and I want you to be the first to hear about it.'

Carl stirred lazily and nibbled her ear. 'Do we have to talk?' he asked.

Kelley kissed him and gently pushed him away. 'I'd like your opinion, Carl,' she said. 'After all, you're the expert.'

He sat up and leaned away from her. 'Come on then. Spill the beans. I'll get no peace till you do.'

She jumped up and fetched her

notebook. She hadn't dared use his computer again, but she'd rewritten her notes. She handed the notebook to him, but she didn't give him a chance to read. Instead she breathlessly outlined her ideas for a new show to follow the life of the *Land Girls* after the war.

'I've been reading up about it. There was such a lot going on — lots of scope for different stories. It doesn't have to all take place in the country. Most of the girls would have gone back to the city to pick up their old lives.' The words tumbled over themselves in her eagerness to impress him.

His expression was unreadable. 'What brought this on?' he asked.

'It just came to me. I was worrying about finding work when *Land Girls* finishes and thinking what a pity it had to end. Then I thought, it doesn't have to end just because the war did.'

'So that's what you were doing on the computer. I didn't realise my Kelley was so clever. But I'd really rather you'd asked before letting yourself into my study.'

Did Kelley imagine it, or did his eyes harden for a fraction of a second before he smiled again, pulling her to him and turning her bones to water with his caresses?

Much later she realised she still hadn't told him about Paul's interview. But it was so hard to get time alone with him. He was always so busy, and when they were together he didn't want to talk.

She lived for the moments spent in his arms and hesitated to spoil the time they had together by talking about something that would upset him. She never questioned him about the future, dreading the frown of irritation and that imperceptible narrowing of his eyes if she mentioned Angela or the divorce.

⋆　⋆　⋆

Sitting alone in the flat one day, she realised she was lonely. She went to the fridge and rummaged for something to eat. But she wasn't really hungry. She made herself coffee instead, but instead of drinking it she decided to call on Marie. Her hair needed re-touching, which gave her a good excuse. It was time she visited her aunt anyway.

After phoning for an appointment, she walked briskly along the river walk, reflecting on her changing relationship with Carl. She hated their times apart and welcomed him eagerly when he returned to the apartment. Their lovemaking was as passionate as ever. But was that it? Trying to be honest with herself, she owned up that it certainly seemed to be, on Carl's part at least.

When they'd first got together they'd talked a lot. He'd taken an interest in her career and seemed to welcome her ideas and suggestions. Now he fobbed her off, becoming impatient if she persisted, or covering her mouth with his and telling her not to waste their precious time together.

But she loved him and would do anything to keep him happy, even if meant giving up any pretence of a so-called normal life. But love should be a two-way affair of give and take, she thought, as she walked briskly towards the Underground station.

At Marie's salon her aunt greeted her with a return of her old exuberance, enfolding Kelley in a huge hug. 'It's good to see you, love. It's been too long.'

Tears threatened once more but Kelley successfully held them at bay. She couldn't let Marie see how fragile her happiness was. *Good job I'm an actress*, she thought, returning the kiss and smiling widely. 'Am I forgiven?' she asked lightly.

'There's nothing to forgive, love. We both said things we shouldn't have. I'm an interfering old busybody and should mind my own business.' She studied Kelley critically, holding her at arm's length, her face serious. 'So long as you're happy, dear, that's all that matters.'

'I am,' Kelley said simply as Marie led her over to the sink and beckoned a girl to wash her hair. Marie patted her shoulder. 'We'll talk later, love.'

When her hair was dry, Kelley touched the lightened strands and smiled cynically. Carl was known for fancying blondes. She wondered what his reaction would be if he ever realised it wasn't her natural colour. Since she'd met him, she'd never given it a chance to grow out.

Marie came over. 'That's better. You were looking a bit pale. Is everything all right?'

'Yes, Auntie. Don't fuss.'

'All right, love. Now, come upstairs. We can't chat properly down here.' She led Kelley up to the flat. She made tea and handed her a plate of biscuits. 'Eat up, love. You're looking a bit thin. Are you sure you're looking after yourself?'

Kelley thought about the huge meals she cooked for Carl and his comments about her weight. 'I'm not thin,' she protested. 'In fact I really ought to go on a diet.'

'Nonsense. You young girls are all the same.' Marie bit into a chocolate digestive and urged Kelley to do the same. With a resigned smile she followed her aunt's example, resolving not to eat dinner that night to make up for it.

'Why don't you and Harry come over for a meal one evening? You haven't seen my new flat yet,' she said.

Marie looked hard at her. 'I might come. But you know Harry doesn't see eye to eye with Carl.'

'Marie, I said *my* flat, not Carl's. He won't be there. He lives on the floor above, when he's there — which isn't often.' Kelley was determined to maintain the fiction that she wasn't actually living with Carl.

'But I thought . . . Harry said . . . '

'I know what you thought despite what I told you. It's true Carl and I love each other and one day, when the time's right, we'll be together. Until then we're trying to do the right thing because his wife's ill and we don't want to hurt her.'

Marie gave a little snort of disbelief but closed her mouth when Kelley gave her a hard look. 'I don't want to fall out with you, but please, try to accept things,' she said.

'I don't want to fight either. It's just that I find it hard to believe Carl Roche is thinking about anyone other than himself. I've known him a lot longer than you have, love. But maybe you're right. Maybe this time he will do the right thing. I hope so for your sake.'

Kelley bit her lip. 'Let's talk about something else. Have you heard from Dad lately?' As soon as the words were out she wished she'd picked another topic. She listened impatiently as Marie gave her another lecture. Then she sighed and promised to phone him when she got home.

As she made her way back to the Underground, she realised she hadn't told Marie about her writing. She'd had another idea and this time she was trying to set it out as a proper script. Perhaps she could sell this one, she thought. Now that she wasn't working regularly, her savings were disappearing fast.

When she got back to River View, Carl's Porsche was in the car park and she hurried to the lift.

As she entered the penthouse he came towards her and grabbed both her hands, gripping them painfully. 'Where have you been?' he snapped.

'Getting my hair done,' she said sharply, pulling away from him.

He looked contrite. 'Sorry, darling, I was worried. You didn't say you were going out.'

She wanted to protest that he hadn't been there to tell, but she forced a smile. 'Marie's done a good job, hasn't she?' she said, touching her hair.

He relaxed and smiled. 'You look great.' He pulled her towards him and kissed her.

'I feel great. Marie and I had a great

time catching up on all the news. Which reminds me, I must ring my dad.' Kelley picked up the phone.

'Not now, darling. I haven't seen you for ages and you haven't said hello to me properly yet. You've had all day to ring your father.'

He held her close and as usual his touch exerted its magic. The phone call went right out of her head.

Later, when he was sleeping, she was annoyed with herself for giving in so easily. It was too late to phone Dad now. She looked down at Carl, wondering why she let him manipulate her. She loved him and wanted to make him happy, but why did she have to do all the giving? It wasn't the first time she'd questioned the way their relationship was going.

She turned away, promising herself that she'd start being more assertive. *It's my life too*, she thought.

First thing in the morning she phoned her father, telling him about the interview she'd done. He sounded pleased for her and he said he'd look out for the magazine. She said goodbye, relieved that Carl's name hadn't cropped up. Apparently Marie had kept her promise not to say anything. She dreaded him finding out she was living with a married man.

Carl came out of the bathroom as she put the phone down. 'Dad OK?' he asked with no trace of the previous evening's resentment.

'He's fine.' Kelley switched on the coffeemaker. 'What are you doing today?' she asked.

'I've got some paperwork to do at home this morning. What about you?'

Kelley shrugged. 'Nothing much.' But she was disappointed. She'd planned to ask Carl if she could use his computer. If only she had her own machine, she could work on her script in secret. She wanted it to be a surprise.

'I'm sure you can amuse yourself while I'm busy. Why not go shopping? You girls love that.' He handed her his gold credit card with a smile. 'Have fun, darling,' he said.

She took the card, although she knew she wouldn't use it. At the door she paused. 'Oh I forgot to ask — did you get round to reading the notes I made for a new series?'

He laughed. 'Don't tell me you were serious about that. I thought it was just a daydream.'

'Of course I was serious. I put a lot of work into it. You were going to read it through and tell me what you thought.'

Carl shrugged again. 'I'd forgotten all about it and I thought you had too. I have had other things on my mind, you know.'

'But what did you think?' Kelley asked eagerly.

'Well, it's not a bad idea and it does have possibilities. But it needs a lot of work. Right now I haven't the time. Why don't we leave it until we know about the new series — then I'll think about it.'

'Can I have my notes back then? I thought I'd work on them, and try to write a proper script. After all, I've nothing to do at the moment. Harry hasn't managed to get any work for me — and you're always busy.'

'I think I threw them away.' Before she could react he said, 'I didn't realise it was so important to you. I'm sorry.'

He seemed genuinely apologetic and Kelley had to accept it, although inwardly she was seething. Why wouldn't he take her seriously?

10

As she sipped her wine and picked at her salad, Kelley felt a warm glow. She'd forgiven Carl for his lack of interest in her project, telling herself that he had a lot on his mind with Angela's illness. It was rare for them to eat out alone and, although he'd looked round carefully to see if any of the paparazzi were lurking, she didn't care.

The evening passed all too quickly and they left the restaurant. When they reached the Porsche, Carl grabbed her, kissing her long and deeply. 'A little appetiser for later,' he murmured.

In the car Kelley leaned back and closed her eyes. He'd been so sweet lately that all her doubts had been swept away. His short temper was natural considering the strain he was under, worrying about Angela, and whether there'd be another series of *Land Girls*.

The next morning she was in the shower and Carl had gone downstairs to get the post and papers. As she stepped out of the cubicle and reached for a towel, he grabbed hold of her, slamming her against the wall.

'What's this?' he roared, pinning her against the wall and waving the newspaper in her face. 'You little slut. You knew they'd be there, you bitch. You planned it, didn't you? Trying to force me into divorcing Angela,' he ranted.

Kelley was too shocked to speak. Obviously something in the paper had set him off.

He released her and she almost fell. Rubbing her shoulder, she found her voice. 'But Paul said . . . '

He wheeled towards her, eyes blazing. This time he didn't shout. His voice was steely. 'Ericson — you've been talking to Ericson. How many times have I told you not to talk to reporters?

God preserve me from brainless bimbos.' He shoved her again and she fell against the washbasin.

She lay trembling until she heard the door slam. She ached all over and she couldn't stop shaking. She dressed slowly, picked up the paper and her bag and crept out.

Downstairs in her flat she sat at the table with her head in her hands, too shaken even to cry. She'd seen Carl's temper many times but she'd never been afraid before. Usually he vented his frustrations by throwing things, but this time she'd really thought he was going to beat her. The scene in the bathroom flooded back and at last the tears came.

When her sobs eased, she splashed her face with cold water at the kitchen sink, then sat at the table and picked up the newspaper, one of the more lurid tabloids.

It was folded back to reveal a picture of herself and Carl, standing beside his Porsche kissing. It must have been taken as they left the restaurant last night. She wondered how the photographer had managed to get so close and why neither she nor Carl had noticed the flash. She smiled grimly. They'd been too wrapped up in each other of course.

Carl was clearly recognisable, as was his car, but her own figure was blurred. There was no mistaking the cascade of long blonde hair down her back, though. Kelley bit her lip, wincing at the headline.

'CARL'S MYSTERY WOMAN'
'Is Carl Roche, noted for his penchant for young blondes, cheating on his wife again? Millionaire Roche, producer/director of the TV series Land Girls, has frequently been seen in the company of beautiful young women. Who is the mystery blonde? Could it be Land Girls star Kelley Robinson, who gossip says has often been seen with Roche?'

Kelley read to the end, her stomach churning. The facts were correct but the way it was written made her squirm. 'Dad,' she gasped. He was sure to see it. She'd have to phone him and reassure him it wasn't her. But would he believe her?

The tabloid had reduced her love for Carl to a sleazy affair. But it wasn't how they'd portrayed it. She rummaged in her bag for Paul Ericson's card. She had something to say to that young man.

When he answered his phone she launched straight into him. 'How could you? I gave you that interview in all good faith. You acted like my friend and I believed you.' She was almost sobbing.

Paul listened in silence. When she ran out of steam he spoke quietly. 'Listen, Kelley, I didn't write it. That interview was for a celeb magazine. Besides, you told me there was nothing between you and Carl Roche — and I believed *you*.'

Kelley drew a shaky breath. Paul

113

seemed sincere. But how could she be sure? Mick Gamble had been furious when she'd thrown them out of her flat. Perhaps he'd followed her, hoping to get his own back by catching her with Carl.

She was a little mollified. 'Anyway, you can't tell it's me from the photo. If it was just a picture I wouldn't mind. It's all the things they said, the innuendoes.'

'Well, just by phoning me you've confirmed it *was* you with Roche. And, I hate to say it, but you should expect this sort of thing when you're in the public eye.'

'But it's not like that. The paper made it sound so — so sleazy,' Kelley wailed.

'And it's not?' Paul gave a cynical laugh. 'I'm surprised at a sensible girl like you getting involved with Roche.'

'Nobody understands,' Kelley said softly, almost in tears.

'It will all blow over in a few days,' Paul said more gently. 'My article will come out next week. That will tell people about the real you.'

Kelley hoped he was right, but as she put the phone down he said, 'You should be more discreet in future if you don't want this to happen again.'

How dare he? It was all his fault in the first place, she thought, slamming the phone down. How could she have been so naive? Paul had seemed so nice, and she'd been completely taken in by him. She wanted to believe him, but who else could it have been? No one knew that she and Carl were lovers. It was her angry reaction when she'd thrown Paul and Mick out of the flat that had confirmed their suspicions.

* * *

Paul put the phone down thoughtfully and stared at his computer screen. He'd been typing up some notes when Kelley rang but now he couldn't concentrate. When he'd realised who it was he'd been too shocked to defend himself.

He felt sorry for her, but he knew from experience it would only be a nine-days' wonder. People would soon find someone else to gossip about. He really hadn't written the story — he didn't write the sort of thing the tabloids printed — but he'd known at once that Mick was responsible.

He thought back to that interview and how agitated Kelley had become when he mentioned Carl. Mick had latched onto it straight away and could hardly contain his fury when they'd been asked to leave.

'She's no better than all these other bits of stuff who shack up with the producer to get on the telly,' he'd snarled as the lift descended.

'I don't think so,' Paul protested mildly. 'She's a nice girl.'

Mick had laughed coarsely. 'Fancy her yourself, do you?'

Paul hadn't replied. But it was true, he thought now, although it was more than that. He felt protective of her. She couldn't know what Carl Roche was really like or she wouldn't be so smitten with him. If she got hurt he hoped he'd be around to help. Meantime he'd have something to say to Mick when they met up again. Not that it would do any good. The tabloids paid well and Mick made no bones about being in it for the money.

Paul was a good journalist and only did the interviews with soap stars and pop singers to pay the bills while he worked on more serious subjects, including the book he was writing about his experiences as a foreign correspondent.

He tried to get back to it but he couldn't settle, and with a groan he switched off the computer, grabbing his leather jacket off the back of the chair. No use trying to get any more work done. He'd call in on Marie. Perhaps he could get her to convince Kelley that the last thing he wanted was to hurt her.

11

Kelley watched as Carl dressed in his weekend clothes, preening in front of the mirror.

'How do I look?' he asked.

'Fantastic, as usual,' Kelley said, her voice flat. She turned away and wandered into the living room.

He followed her. 'What's wrong?' He grabbed her shoulders and turned her to face him. 'Oh, darling, you're still upset, aren't you?' His expression was sombre. 'I've already apologised. What else can I do? I was so angry, I couldn't help lashing out. I'm really, truly sorry.'

'You scared me, Carl.'

'I know, darling. But it won't happen again. Say you've forgiven me.'

She managed a small smile. 'Yes, I've forgiven you, but . . . '

'But what?'

'You're going away again and leaving

me on my own.' She knew she sounded petulant but she couldn't help it. 'What am I going to do with myself all weekend?'

Carl's expression hardened. 'I thought you understood. This weekend's very important to me. I've had the devil's own job getting George to sign this deal, especially after all that stuff in the papers. Luckily Angela believed my version of the story and she's calmed down a bit. I've got to keep her sweet for a bit longer, just till this deal goes through.'

'Of course — the deal,' Kelley said. 'And there I was thinking you were worried about Angela. How is she, by the way? Recovered from her illness yet?' She couldn't keep the sarcasm from her voice.

Carl frowned and passed a hand over his face. 'She's still very frail — the doctors say it'll be a long haul.' He touched her cheek gently. 'Say you understand, darling,' he said. The words were gentle enough, but there was an edge to his voice and his eyes were cold despite his smile.

'Of course, I understand,' Kelley whispered.

'Good girl,' he said, kissing her lightly, good humour restored.

That was when Kelley realised he didn't really love her, not in the way she wanted to be loved. Things hadn't been the same since he'd lost his temper again. He'd calmed down later and now believed that she hadn't engineered the tabloid story. Through his press contacts he'd learned that it was all Mick Gamble's doing. Kelley was relieved that Paul had told the truth. She hadn't wanted to believe that he'd betrayed her.

'In future, you don't talk to the press without clearing it with me or the company's press department,' Carl had told her.

She'd agreed, although she hadn't liked the threatening way he'd enforced his demand. But he was upset and she didn't blame him. After all, she'd been upset too. But then she'd seen Paul's article in the celeb magazine. He'd only used the information she'd given him and since then, her fan mail had increased dramatically. When she'd showed it to Carl, he'd been somewhat mollified.

He was ready to leave now and he put his arms round her, pulling her close. Despite her doubts, she felt the familiar quiver of desire that his touch always produced.

But once he'd gone she paced the apartment restlessly. She ought to get on with her new script, but she couldn't think straight. She couldn't stifle the doubts about their relationship when she was alone.

Today Carl had only seemed concerned about the deal with his father-in-law. Not a word about Angela, until she'd mentioned her health. Although they lived separate lives, Kelley thought he should show more care for the woman he was still married to.

If he really loved me I could put up with the bursts of temper, the vanity, the ruthless ambition, Kelley thought. But if she was honest she had to admit that theirs was just a physical relationship. Was that what she really wanted?

Carl seemed incapable of real love. There had been little in their relationship of the affection, sharing and commitment that had been so much a part of her parents' marriage. Kelley had hoped to find the same fulfilment when she fell in love. But these sentiments seemed alien to Carl. Now, she was beginning to believe the stories about him and wondered why Angela hadn't divorced him long ago.

She stopped pacing and stood by the window. It was no good constantly going over it. She'd talk things over with him when he returned from Lydford. She couldn't carry on like this. Meantime there was no point staying here brooding.

Perhaps she'd go shopping, although it wouldn't be much fun on her own. She still had Carl's credit card, but if she did buy anything she certainly wouldn't use it. But perhaps a trawl round the big stores would help to take her mind off the worrying way their relationship was developing.

She grabbed her bag and a jacket and ran downstairs. Although it was chilly for August with a fine misty drizzle, she scarcely noticed the weather as she hurried towards the Underground station. She was sadly going over the many times Carl had let her down, leaving her to her own devices.

It's my own fault, she told herself, determined to do something about it. She wouldn't spend the rest of her life sitting at home waiting for a man who cared so little about her. It was time to stand up for herself.

She got off the tube at Oxford Circus and hurried up the steps, diving into one of the big stores to get out of the rain. There wasn't anything she really wanted, but she bought a pair of jeans. Carl hated women in jeans but in her new-found spirit of independence she didn't care.

She left the store swinging the carrier bag and walking with a lighter step. If she loved Carl, she'd make allowances for his lapses of temper. After all, he had a lot on his mind with his business problems as well as worrying about Angela. But should she?

Deep in thought, she crossed the road and looked in the window of a large computer store. Since college she'd had little interest in technology, scorning the gadgets that everyone deemed essential these days. Even her mobile phone was very basic, a Christmas present from her father 'so that you can keep in touch', he had said with a wistful smile.

She had intended to seek Carl's advice before buying herself a laptop, but she was here now and who better to ask than one of the knowledgeable assistants in the store.

Inside she paused, bewildered by the vast array of brightly lit screens and the shelves full of gadgets that she'd had no idea even existed. It was as if she'd been living in a bubble since she'd moved in with Carl, while the rest of the world moved on without her.

A young man who looked as if he should still be in school came towards her and asked, 'How may I help you?'

Kelley was completely out of her depth. 'I need a laptop — I think,' she stammered.

'What do you have at the moment? Do you want to part exchange?' he asked.

'I don't have one.'

'Your PC then? You'll need something compatible. What internet package do you use?'

The questions came so thick and fast that Kelley was lost for words. 'I'm really not sure. Perhaps I could come back another time.' She'd ask Erica or one of the others to come with her.

'Well, while you're here, why not have a look at some of the display models?' the assistant said.

'No, I'll leave it, thank you.'

As she turned away, someone called

her and she turned to face Paul Ericson.

'Kelley, it *is* you. What are you doing here?'

She hadn't spoken to him since that phone call and, knowing that Carl mistrusted him, she was reluctant to chat. But she really liked him, and besides, there was no news value in her being in a computer store — alone.

Nevertheless, she glanced round to make sure his mate Mick wasn't lurking in the background, then smiled and said, 'Hello, Paul. I could ask you the same.'

He grinned. 'Pure coincidence, Kelley. I'm getting some new printer cartridges.'

The assistant, who was still hovering nearby, said, 'The lady wants a laptop, but she can't decide.'

'Would you like me to help you choose?' Paul asked.

Although reluctant to expose her ignorance, Kelley decided she'd prefer his advice to that of the eager assistant, who would probably confuse her with all the technical jargon. So she smiled and said, 'If you've got time, I'd be grateful.'

During the next half hour Paul took her through the laptop section, explaining the merits or otherwise of each model. He knew his stuff and with his help she made up her mind.

'It's got wi-fi so you can do all sorts of things on it,' Paul said, laughing at her expression.

Patiently he explained and Kelley said, 'But I only want it for writing stuff.' She blushed, fearful of being ridiculed, especially as Paul was a writer.

But he merely smiled. 'Well, you can use it for email and the internet and Facebook. You'll need a printer, too, if you're writing stuff.'

He selected a not-too-expensive model and as they waited for the assistant to process Kelley's credit card, he said, 'What are you writing, if you don't mind me asking?'

She hesitated for a moment before

blurting it out. 'I've had an idea for a TV series. I thought I'd try to work up a script.'

Paul didn't laugh or dismiss the idea as she'd feared. 'Have you done anything like this before?' he asked.

She shook her head. 'As I said, it's just an idea. I don't know the first thing about script-writing, but I've seen enough of them lately . . . ' Her voice trailed off and she laughed self-consciously.

The assistant put the laptop and printer in a bag and handed her the receipt. She thanked him and started for the door.

Outside she said, 'Thanks for your help, Paul. I can't wait to get home and start using this.'

'Do you have to rush off? I'd like to hear about this idea of yours. Perhaps we could go for a coffee.'

She hesitated. Suppose someone saw them together and told Carl? He'd be furious. Stupid, she told herself. This was the middle of London — no one who knew them within miles.

Before she could accept, Paul said with a laugh, 'I promise I won't write about you — not without your consent anyway.'

'I wasn't worried about that,' Kelley said, giggling. 'Yes, please. I would like a coffee.'

Paul led her down a side street to a small café. 'This is better than the chain coffee shops,' he said, pulling out a chair for her. While he ordered, Kelley looked round appreciatively. The café was done out in a retro style and reminded her of the place on the seafront in Holton where she and her friends had hung out after school.

They settled with their drinks and Paul said, 'I love Harry and Marie's parties, but it's nice to be able to sit and chat quietly for a change.'

'I'm not one for partying myself,' Kelley said.

'I noticed — you always seem to disappear halfway through the evening.' He stirred his coffee and was silent for a moment. 'So, how are things going with *Land Girls*? I hear this is the last series. What will you do next?'

She hesitated. 'Well, if no acting jobs turn up, I might try my hand at script-writing.'

'What's this idea you've got?'

'I don't know. It's nothing special.' Kelley wasn't sure if she wanted to share her idea and she wished she hadn't mentioned it in the first place. Much as she was beginning to like Paul, she still wasn't entirely sure she could trust him.

He seemed to sense her feelings and he leaned across the table and took her hand. 'You don't have to tell me. I understand. I don't like talking about my writing projects either.'

She pulled her hand away and took a sip of her coffee. Could she confide in him? But he was a writer and he'd tell her if she was wasting her time. She took a deep breath. 'It's for a follow-up series to *Land Girls* — about what happens to the characters after the war.'

'Sounds good. Tell me more.'

Paul seemed genuinely interested and she found herself gushing in her eagerness to outline the storylines she'd dreamed up. She finally ran out of steam and looked up at him with an embarrassed smile. 'Sorry for going on. I hope I haven't bored you,' she said.

'Not at all. It sounds great.' He gestured towards the bag containing the laptop. 'You'd better get writing then.'

'Do you really think so?'

'Don't see why not. Have you talked to Carl about it?'

'I showed him my notes ages ago but he didn't seem interested. He hasn't mentioned it since. Of course, he's always so busy, so . . .'

'Well, if he doesn't like it there are other producers,' Paul said.

Kelley stood up and shrugged on her jacket. 'Well, as you said, better get home and start writing — trouble is, I'm such a novice. I know what a script looks like of course, but I'm wondering if I remember enough word processing from college to type it up properly.'

'There are programmes you can download from the internet,' Paul said. He tore a page out of his notebook and scribbled. 'Here's the one I use.'

She thanked him and they parted at the entrance to the tube station. Back in the flat Kelley was excited at the prospect of a new challenge and with a start, she realised she'd hardly thought about Carl for hours.

She glanced at the clock. He was due back that evening, but there was time to try out her new toy before showering and going up to the penthouse.

Before unpacking the laptop though, she decided to phone her father. She felt a little guilty that she'd rather neglected him lately. He seemed pleased to hear from her but she thought he sounded tired. 'I'll be down to see you at the weekend,' she promised before ringing off.

It took her ages to set up the laptop and download the programme Paul had recommended. She got her rough notes out of the drawer and was about to sit down at the computer when she heard the lift.

Was Carl back already? He'd expect her to be waiting for him, dressed and ready to celebrate the success of his latest business deal — or to drown their sorrows if it had not gone according to plan.

She switched off the machine and rushed into the bedroom, slipping out of her jeans and t-shirt and grabbing a dress off the hanger. After running a comb through her hair, she dashed on some lipstick and ran up to the penthouse.

Carl was pacing the room, a look of fury on his handsome face. Before she had a chance to apologise, he rounded on her. 'Where the hell have you been?' he shouted, raising his hand.

She flinched away from his fist, although he didn't hit her. 'I was downstairs getting ready. I didn't hear you come in,' she stammered.

'What have you been up to all

weekend?' he ranted. 'Is it too much to ask that you be here when I get home?'

The injustice of it stung and tears welled up. He was always off somewhere, and how was she to know when he was coming back if he never so much as sent her a text? 'I'm sorry, Carl. I didn't notice the time.' She stammered her apology, her voice choking on a sob.

His fury evaporated immediately at the sight of her tears and he moved towards her, contrition on his face. 'Kelley, darling, I'm sorry. It's just — I was so worried when you weren't here. I thought you'd left me.' He took her in his arms, working his usual magic with his touch.

Almost against her will, she succumbed to his embrace. 'I won't leave you,' she whispered.

Later, Carl ordered a take-away, saying he was too tired to go out. Kelley didn't mind. She was getting fed up with Carl's paranoia about being seen with her.

As soon as they'd finished eating, she

leapt up and started to clear away the empty dishes, but Carl put his hand on her arm.

'Leave that for a moment,' he said.

Kelley was surprised, knowing how Carl hated to sit surrounded by the debris of a meal. She paused with a plate in her hand, her stomach beginning to churn as she wondered if she'd upset him again.

'Tell me what you've been up to while I was away,' he said, patting the sofa beside him and gesturing her to sit.

She swallowed and summoned a smile. 'I went shopping,' she said.

He laughed. 'Spending all my money, eh?'

'Not this time. I bought a laptop.'

'Whatever for? Do you even know how to use it?'

'Of course — I did computers at college before I came to London.'

His eyes narrowed. 'Oh, yes. I remember now — you used my computer, didn't you.'

'Carl, I've apologised for that — and

I haven't touched it since.' She mentally crossed her fingers. She had switched it on once, just to print off the notes she'd typed. But she hadn't been able to find the file and assumed she'd deleted it by mistake. Since then she hadn't set foot in Carl's study.

'I believe you, darling,' he said, running his fingers down her spine. 'So, why a laptop?'

She moved away, not wanting to be distracted. 'I have so much time on my hands when you're away. I wanted something to do. I'm writing a script,' she said.

He started to laugh. 'So you were serious about that, were you?'

'Of course. I showed you my notes.'

'So you did. And I said I'd give it some thought. It was just a few scribbled ideas, wasn't it? I'm not sure if it would work, coming so soon after *Land Girls*. Perhaps the public wants something different now.'

'I thought with such popular characters, a follow-up series made sense.'

Although disappointed with his reaction, she wasn't ready to give up. 'Carl, if I write something, at least have a look at it. I'd really value your opinion.'

'Have you spoken to anyone else about this — your aunt or old Levinson?'

'Not a word,' Kelley said. She wasn't about to confess that she'd discussed it with Paul, knowing how he felt about the journalist.

'Well, when you have a draft script, let me see it. I'll think about it.'

Kelley threw her arms round him. 'Thank you, thank you.' She kissed him and murmured, 'I do love you, Carl.'

He kissed her back hungrily and she melted into him, firmly pushing to the back of her mind that earlier moment of threatened violence and her resolve to be more assertive.

12

Carl's mood seemed to have improved lately, Kelley thought. Perhaps she was learning what was likely to upset him and merely avoiding confrontations. Or maybe he was happier since he'd finalised the deal with his father-in-law and added another brick to his growing empire.

When they were at River View, he often joined the cast for drinks after the day's shooting, although he never singled Kelley out. Still, she noticed the pointed looks when he offered her a lift home at the end of the evening. But, as she said to Erica, 'We live in the same building so . . . '

She managed to find time to work on her script, which had the provisional title of *Going Home*. The first episode dealt with the end of the war and the Land Girls' plans for the future.

Drawing on memories of her parents starting their village shop when her father had come out of the army, she had written an episode with Violet and her boyfriend doing the same. She knew that many of the returning soldiers and airmen had found it difficult to adjust after their wartime experiences, and this would provide the conflict in the ongoing story.

She had been typing for most of the morning and had reached the end of the last scene. She saved it and did a backup copy, putting the memory stick in a zipped pocket of her handbag. She placed the printout in the folder containing her *Land Girls* script. She'd show it to Carl later. She was excited about it and longed to tell Erica. But he'd warned her to keep quiet until he had secured backing for the series.

★　★　★

Kelley was enjoying spending more time with Carl since the break in filming. He'd been taking her on leisurely drives in the countryside, stopping at remote country pubs and often staying the night.

That weekend they'd found a little pub not far from her home village. As they lazed in front of the log fire, she asked Carl if they could call in at the shop before returning to London. She hadn't spoken to her father lately and felt bad for neglecting him.

Before she could speak Carl said, 'Have you done anything more about that script we spoke of?' he asked.

'I've finished the first episode. I was going to show it to you when we get back. I'll bring the printout with me to work on Monday.'

'Have you done a backup?' he asked.

Proud of her new-found computer savvy, she said, 'It's on a memory stick.' Unconsciously, she patted the handbag at the side of her chair.

Carl smiled and leaned forward to take her hand. 'Enough of business talk,' he said. 'I think it's time for bed.'

It wasn't until they got back to London that she remembered her intention to visit her father. She'd have to ring him later and try to go down next week.

★   ★   ★

Carl didn't mention her script again and she didn't like to pester him about it. Besides, it needed more work. Since finishing it, she'd thought of a couple of improvements to the story and she'd also come up with another series idea. But there'd been no time to develop now that they were filming again.

They'd just finished a scene and Simon called for a break. 'Let's hope the weather holds for Norfolk, folks. Meanwhile it's the final indoor scenes tomorrow.' He handed out copies of the shooting schedule. 'Don't be late — there's a lot to get through.'

The group broke up and some of them suggested going for a drink.

Kelley looked round for Carl, but he hadn't returned from his meeting, so she declined, ignoring the knowing looks which passed between Judy and Phil.

She went up to her flat and changed, then ran up the stairs to the penthouse, hoping that Carl had come back while she was showering. But the room was empty. She picked up a copy of *Film and Television* magazine from the coffee table and sat down to wait for him.

As she idly flicked through the pages, a picture of Carl caught her eye. She was so used to seeing his photo that she almost turned the page without reading, until the headline caught her eye. Her eyes widened in disbelief. Why hadn't he said anything? And why wasn't her name mentioned?

* * *

When Carl put his key in the lock he was whistling under his breath. 'Hello, darling, I've got good news,' he said cheerfully.

She looked at him coldly. 'You rat,' she said, thrusting the magazine at him.

His eyes narrowed but he recovered immediately. 'I hoped you wouldn't see that before I'd had a chance to explain,' he said smoothly.

'What is there to explain? You know how much work I put into it; how much it meant to me. But you've gone ahead and put it about that it's all your idea. No credit to me at all. How could you?'

'Kelley, darling, it's not like that. I meant to tell you. And you will get the credit. Your name will be up there when the show goes out.'

'But why doesn't it say so in this article? It's all the great Carl Roche and his marvellous new series that's going to do even better than *Land Girls*. Not a word about it being my idea.'

She picked up her coffee mug and went through to the kitchen.

He followed her and leaned against

the worktop, but she kept her back to him.

'Don't take it like that, Kelley. I always meant for you to have the credit. You know what these reporters are like. They twist everything. I thought you'd be pleased. We've got funding for the final series of *Land Girls* and this will follow on.'

'I am pleased. But you haven't even seen the complete script. I thought you'd discuss it with me first.'

'But you were still working on it. Besides, I had your original notes, which is all we need at this stage.'

'So, who else knows about this — apart from the writer of this article and everyone else in show business?'

'I've discussed it with Simon — I'd like him to direct. But it's a long way off. We'll have to wait and see the ratings for *Land Girls* first.' He pulled her towards him. 'Come on, darling, there's no need to be upset. You'll get the credit.' He stroked her hair, his hand straying down to slip the strap of her dress off her shoulder.

Oh no, he wouldn't get round her that easily. She pushed him away. 'Carl, I don't just want a credit. I want to be involved. I know I'm not that experienced, but I know I can do it.'

His lips curled in a sneer. 'It's not as easy as that. There's a lot more to producing a series than just the script. I suppose you'll be wanting to direct as well.'

'And why not?' she demanded, eyes flashing.

'Because you're an actress, Kelley. My credibility would fly out of the window if I let you loose on it.' He reached for her again. 'Let's not fight, darling. I've been so busy lately. I was hoping for a little relaxation when I got home.'

'Yes, that's all you want me for. Well, I'm not just a brainless blonde with no mind of her own. I'm ambitious too.'

'I've discovered that. No doubt moving in with me was just a career move. You're just like all the others,

Kelley. But you can't manipulate me. I've got a lot of power in the television industry,' he said.

Her eyes flashed. 'Are you threatening me? That's it, then — I'm leaving.' She turned on her heel and marched into the bedroom. As she threw open cupboards and drawers, throwing her things into a holdall, Carl stood in the doorway and watched.

'Darling, please don't go,' he said, a catch in his voice.

She threw him a stony look and carried on packing. When she returned to the living room he was sitting by the window, his head in his hands.

'I'll clear my flat later on. And here's the key to this place.' She fumbled in her handbag and held it out to him.

He made no move to take it, just looked up at her quickly and dropped his head in his hands again. She put the key on the table and said softly, 'I'm sorry it had to end like this.'

He looked up. 'So am I.' As she turned away he grabbed her hand. 'I don't want you to go, Kelley,' he said, grasping her hand tighter. 'Please, give me another chance.'

She knelt beside him. 'Oh, Carl, why do I let you get round me like this?'

He pulled her close and kissed her lingeringly. Almost against her will, she submitted, even as a small voice in her head told her she was making a big mistake.

★   ★   ★

'There's no copyright on ideas love,' Harry said when she went to see him next day. 'Let's have a look.'

While he read the printout she sat twisting her fingers together. She and Carl had made up their quarrel in the usual way and he'd promised to give her credit for her script. To all outward appearances everything was fine between them now, but she still didn't entirely trust him.

Hating herself for her disloyalty, she'd decided to ask Harry's advice.

This was her baby and she wasn't going to let Carl take the credit without a fight.

'This is good, love. I can understand Carl wanting it,' Harry said, but his next words were like a deluge of cold water. 'But I'm sorry, love. You don't have a leg to stand on unless he copies your script word for word. And there's nothing on this printout to say who wrote it. Is it on your computer?'

'I thought I'd saved it but it's disappeared.'

Harry smiled grimly. 'Perhaps someone deleted it on purpose,' he said.

'Oh I'm sure Carl wouldn't do anything like that,' she protested. But her voice lacked conviction. She still had her doubts.

'What about a backup?'

'It's here.' She rummaged through her bag but it wasn't there. 'It must be back at the flat,' she said.

'You sure?'

Kelley shook her head, wishing she'd taken more care. 'At least I've got the printout,' she said.

'I'm sorry I can't help, love.' Harry gave her a hug. 'At least, using the same characters, there'll be a part in the new series for you.'

'I hope so. The pilot episode is about Violet setting up in business after the war. You think it's a good idea, don't you, Harry?'

'Yes, and so did Carl. Otherwise he wouldn't have pinched it.'

'He wasn't that keen when I first mentioned it. I couldn't believe it when I saw that article.'

'Next time keep it under your hat.' Harry opened the door and followed her downstairs. As they reached the street he said, 'You should carry on writing. You're good. And if there's no acting, you can write while you're 'resting'.'

Kelley laughed. 'Beats cleaning up the salon or working in Dad's shop,' she said.

'Seriously though, love. If you get any more good ideas, keep them to yourself

— and do a backup,' Harry said as they parted on the corner.

'Don't worry, I will. I'm already working on another one.'

She said goodbye and hurried down the steps to the Underground. Harry's down-to-earth common sense had cheered her up, but she didn't know how she felt about Carl now. It was easy to be dispassionate when they were apart, but she knew he only had to reach out and take her in his arms, and once more she was lost.

13

Carl had gone down to Lydford again and Kelley was feeling resentful. When she'd protested, he explained that Angela's father had promised to put up the money for the new series. If he found out that Carl was having an affair, the deal would be off.

Kelley hated it when he was away. Since she'd threatened to leave him, he seemed to have been making an effort to please her. But did she still love him? Surely, once he'd sorted out the problems with his wife, everything would come right for them.

When we're working together on the new programme, we'll be proper partners, she thought, gazing out of the window at the sluggish waters of the Thames. But deep down she knew it wouldn't be like that. Carl had to be in control. And she had to ask herself if she was prepared to continue in such a one-sided relationship.

Her thoughts were interrupted by the telephone. She leapt towards it, thinking — hoping — it was Carl.

Her smile faded as a woman's voice asked for Miss Robinson. 'My name's Rowena Sheridan. I'm a researcher for *London Tonight*. How do you feel about a spot on the show with Bruce Clark?'

Kelley's first reaction was a leap of excitement. Any actress would give the earth for an interview with Bruce Clark.

'That's wonderful,' she said. But what would Carl say? she wondered. She couldn't go through all that again. On a live television show it could be even worse, especially if Bruce Clark decided to start probing her private life. Carl would be furious. But why should she worry what Carl said?

Rowena set up the time and date and a few evenings later found her sitting on the famous red sofa in the *London*

Tonight studio. She was a bundle of nerves. It was different when you had a script, she thought. But, despite her apprehension, she began to relax as Bruce questioned her about her start in acting and her part in the series. There was only one moment when she wished it could have gone differently — when Bruce mentioned *Going Home*. 'Do you think it'll be as successful as *Land Girls*?' he asked.

'I'm sure it will.' Kelley was about to go on and explain her involvement but Bruce interrupted.

'Carl Roche's productions do have a habit of hitting the jackpot,' he said. 'Well, that's all we've got time for. Thank you for being on the show.'

The familiar *London Tonight* music started up and the audience began to applaud. It was too late to set the record straight. Kelley bit her lip as the lights faded. At least Carl would be happy, she thought. She knew he'd be watching.

In the taxi, Kelley reflected that it

was probably just as well she hadn't been able to talk about the series. It might have provoked awkward questions about her relationship with Carl.

The next day, on the train going up to Norwich, she went over the previous evening's conversation with him. He'd been pleased with her appearance on Bruce's show, but when she'd mentioned the new series, he'd silenced her with a kiss.

'I told you, darling. You'll get the credit,' he said, sweeping her into his arms.

But she hadn't really been reassured. The train pulled into Norwich Thorpe station and she closed her laptop, wondering if she'd have time to pop into a computer shop in the city to buy another memory stick. She was still annoyed with herself for losing the other one. It had taken ages to type the script again.

She hadn't really minded when Carl said he wouldn't be able to join the crew till later in the week. Time away from him would give her time to reassess their relationship. She was beginning to realise he wasn't the man she'd thought he was. Oh yes, he could still lay on the charm, and of course there was the physical attraction too. But was that all she wanted in a relationship?

She couldn't forget the times when his temper had exploded so ferociously. *I can forgive, but I can't forget*, she thought. Now that little ripple of fear was always there — and she couldn't live with a man she was afraid of. But could she leave him, she wondered, remembering his vulnerability when she'd almost walked out.

I never thought I'd be relieved to get away from him, she thought, taking a deep breath as she spotted Simon waving across the barrier. She shook off her dark thoughts and greeted the director with a smile.

'It's so good of you to come and meet me,' she said.

'Orders from the boss,' he said,

taking her bag. 'Come on, let's get out of this rain.'

They dashed across the car park and were soon leaving the busy roads around Norwich behind. The countryside didn't look quite so appealing today, shrouded in mist, the trees drooping under the weight of the heavy downpour. But Kelley gave a sigh of contentment. It was so good to get away from London — and Carl, she added silently.

★　★　★

Despite the dreadful weather, shooting went reasonably well. Strong winds and driving rain kept them indoors some of the time, but Simon and Mark, the scriptwriter, huddled together and adapted the storyline to fit the conditions. It added to the drama and everyone was happy when they wrapped up on the last day. There were just a few indoor scenes to shoot back in London and the series would be finished.

In the snug bar of the pub, celebrating the successful wrap, Kelley was enjoying herself when the door opened and Paul came in. What was he doing here? She hadn't seen him since buying the laptop.

She waved and he pushed his way through the crowded bar.

'Nice to see you again, Kelley,' he said when he reached her. 'I just want a quick word with Simon. Can I buy you a drink later?'

She nodded and sipped her white wine. The noise in the bar was deafening.

She was laughing at one of Phil's jokes when her mobile rang. *It must be Carl*, she thought, tempted to ignore the call. She checked anyway but it wasn't him and she didn't recognise the number.

Her heart began a slow thumping when she heard her aunt's voice. 'Marie — what's wrong?' She felt queasy. Marie wouldn't phone unless it was urgent. 'Is it Harry?'

Marie sounded unusually subdued. 'No, Kelley, love. It's your dad.'

'Oh, no . . . '

'He's in intensive care — a heart attack. Can you get down here?'

'I don't know. It's late — no trains. What shall I do?' her voice broke.

'Try to keep calm, love,' Marie said. 'Why not hire a car?'

'Good idea. I'll meet you at the hospital.' She switched the phone off, trying to still the trembling in her legs, and went through to the bar.

The landlord was busy serving and she started to cry.

Paul rushed over. 'What's wrong? Has someone upset you?'

'I need a car. My dad's been taken ill,' she said, clutching his sleeve.

'But it's nearly midnight. I'm going back to London in the morning — I'll take you then,' he said.

Simon butted in. 'Do you have to go? It'll play havoc with the shooting schedules,' he said.

Paul glared. 'Can't you see she's had

a shock? The last thing on her mind right now is your blasted schedule. Go and get her a brandy or something for God's sake.' He put an arm round Kelley's shoulder and forced her into a chair. 'Don't worry, they'll sort something out. Now sit here for a minute.'

Simon brought the brandy over and persuaded her to take a sip. She shuddered as it went down but the trembling stopped. 'I must go,' she said and tried to stand.

Paul put out a restraining hand. 'I'll drive you. Finish your brandy.'

As she sipped the comforting liquor, Simon sat beside her scrawling on his clipboard. He patted her arm. 'Sorry, pet. That was insensitive of me. Don't worry — I'll rearrange tomorrow's schedule. And if you need to be gone a few days I'll get Mark to do a bit of a rewrite.' He gave her a hug. 'Now you get off, pet.'

Kelley smiled gratefully. 'I'm sorry to let you down. But I really must go.'

'I understand. Don't worry, pet. Give

us a ring when you know what's happening. I'll let Carl know too, but I'm sure he'll understand.'

Kelley gave him a hug and followed Paul out to the car park. As she settled into the ramshackle old Volkswagen and snapped the seat-belt on, she reflected that she hadn't even spared Carl a thought. All that mattered was getting to Dad and letting him know that in spite of everything she loved him. Before it was too late.

Paul tried to make small talk, but when Kelley didn't reply he fell silent. He glanced across at her. 'I know it's easy to say, but you should try and relax. Put the seat back a bit and try to sleep. You're going to need your strength when we get there.'

As the car purred on through the night, Kelley gazed tensely out of the window, although there was nothing to see. Against her will, her eyes closed, lulled by the rhythm of the car's movement and the soft music which Paul had switched on.

The slowing of the car brought her awake with a jerk. She couldn't believe she'd slept. 'Here already?' she asked.

'Yes, thank goodness for sat nav.' Paul pulled up in front of the main entrance. 'I'll go and find a parking space, catch up with you later.'

Kelley didn't reply. She leapt out of the car and raced inside. Marie was sitting in the waiting area, leaning back with her eyes closed. She jumped up when Kelley addressed her.

'Is Dad all right? What's happening?' Kelley gasped.

Marie tried to smile. 'It's bad, love. They say he's stabilised but he's very weak.'

'I must see him,' Kelley sobbed. Marie put her arm round her and looked up as Paul joined them.

'Thanks for driving her down. Be a love and try to find a doctor or somebody; tell them Mr Robinson's daughter's here.'

Paul disappeared, returning a few moments later with a nurse who showed them to the intensive care unit. 'I can only let his daughter go in,' she said.

Holding her breath, Kelley followed her into the little room. Was that really her father? He seemed to have shrunk, his eyes sunk in deep hollows, his skin grey and clammy. Wires and tubes trailed from the bed to the array of apparatus beside it. Green dots bounced their way across the screen, giving off a faint bleep.

'You can stay for a few minutes,' the sister said and left her alone.

Kelley pulled up a chair, sat down and took her father's hand gently. It was as cold as ice. She leaned over him, willing herself to see the faint rise and fall of the blanket which showed he was still breathing.

'Dad, I'm sorry,' she whispered. Then as the tears fell freely, 'Please don't die.'

His eyes flickered open and his lips twisted in a smile. 'You came,' he gasped.

'Oh, Dad.' The tears fell more freely.

'Don't cry, sweetheart, please.'

She dashed her hand across her eyes. 'Just get well, Dad, please.'

The effort to speak had tired him and his eyes closed once more. She sat holding his hand, praying that he would rally. Her eyelids drooped and she willed herself to stay awake. She had no idea how long she sat there.

Marie came in once and put her hand on her shoulder, giving a comforting pat. Her father was still unconscious, his face grey. Suddenly his laboured breath stopped and the machine at his bedside started to beep.

'Dad, Dad!' Kelley cried. 'Nurse, someone, please come quickly!'

The room was full of people and Kelley was ushered outside. Marie folded her in her arms and Paul gave an encouraging smile, but it was no comfort. Dad was gone before she'd had the chance to make up for her neglect of him.

It was getting light when they reached the shop where Kelley had grown up. She couldn't help noticing that it looked even more run-down and shabby than on her previous visit.

Paul hesitated at the front door. 'I ought to get back to London,' he said.

'Nonsense,' said Marie. 'You can't do any more driving tonight.'

'She's right,' said Kelley. 'I'll make up a bed for you on the sofa. Marie, you can have my old room.' Having something to do helped, but she couldn't get that image of her father's waxy face out of her mind.

'What about you, love? You ought to get some rest,' Marie said.

'I don't think I can sleep.' She made a pot of tea and sat at the kitchen table, looking round at the familiar room, which hadn't changed since her mother had died. Dad had always been too busy with the shop to worry about decorating, and lately he just couldn't be bothered anyway.

A wave of guilt swept over her as she realised he must have been ill for some time. She should have noticed there was something wrong on her last visit. Instead she had been so wrapped up in Carl as well as her career, she'd had no time for him. She dropped her head on her folded arms and wept.

She must have dozed off when the storm of weeping stopped, and she sat up with a jerk when Paul touched her shoulder, realising that it was morning.

'I must make a move soon. I have to get back to London,' he said.

Kelley sat up and rubbed her red, swollen eyes. She went to the kitchen sink and bathed her face with cold water. Running her fingers through her hair, she tried to smile at Paul. 'You must've been so uncomfortable on that old sofa. I hope you managed to get a bit of sleep.'

'I was so tired I could have slept on the bare floor. What about you? I don't think you went to bed at all, did you?'

Kelley shook her head. 'I just kept seeing my dad lying there with all those wires and things.'

Paul took her hand. 'I'm so sorry.'

Marie came downstairs, rubbing her eyes. 'Still here, young man?' she said.

Paul grinned. 'Couldn't leave without saying goodbye to my favourite lady,' he said.

'And you can't leave without having something to eat,' she said.

She busied herself at the stove while Kelley went through to the shop. She'd have to let the post office people know about Dad. His assistant, Mrs Briggs, would be here soon. She'd been the one who called the ambulance and found Marie's phone number.

When she heard the news, her face creased in concern. 'Oh, Kelley, love. I'm so sorry. Did you get here in time?'

Kelley nodded.

'Well, don't worry about anything, dear. I'll keep things ticking over until we know what's what. And I'll try to arrange for a temporary post office assistant.'

'Thank you, Mrs Briggs.'

'Katy, please,' she said, giving Kelley's shoulder a pat. 'Now I'd better get on. We'll have the school kids in any minute now.'

When Kelley went into the back room, Marie was just dishing up some scrambled eggs. 'Sit down, love. You must eat.'

'I don't think I can,' Kelley said. But when Marie placed the plate in front of her, she realised how hungry she was.

While they ate Paul told her he'd gone to Norfolk to see Simon, who'd been offered a directing job in Hollywood. 'He's promised me an exclusive interview when and if he does take up the offer,' Paul said.

Kelley realised he was trying to take her mind off her father and tried to concentrate. 'But he can't go. I thought he was going to direct the new show,' Kelley said.

'Well, he hasn't decided yet. But keep it quiet, won't you? I promised not to write anything until he gives me the go-ahead. And I always keep my word,' he said.

Kelley felt herself flush, but she

didn't reply. When she looked up from her plate, Paul was smiling at her. Almost against her will she smiled back.

When they'd finished eating Kelley went up to shower and change, and as she came downstairs her mobile rang. Before she could speak, Carl's voice blasted in her ear.

'What the hell do you think you're playing at, Kelley? Don't you realise you can't just walk off the set and leave everyone in the lurch like that? I've just arrived to find you gone.'

Kelley's stomach churned but she answered evenly, 'My father has just died. I hardly think that could be described as *playing* at anything.'

Carl reacted as if he hadn't heard. 'You'll be in breach of your contract if you don't get back here right away. Don't you realise we're losing money waiting on you?'

'I don't care. I have too much else to think about right now,' Kelley said, on the verge of tears.

'That's not a very professional

attitude,' Carl said, his voice cold. 'And what about letting the others down? Doesn't that worry you?'

'I'm not letting anyone down. Simon said he'd adjust the schedules and get Mark to do some rewriting. He said you'd understand.' Kelley dashed away a stray tear from her cheek. 'I thought you would too,' she said in a small voice.

Carl's voice softened. 'I'm sorry, darling. But I've got a lot of money tied up in this show, contracts and that. Oh well, I can let you have a couple of days I suppose,' he said carelessly.

'I might need more than a couple of days. There's the funeral to organise, and the shop . . . I just don't know when I'll get back.'

'And you were the one who talked about commitment,' Carl said, and Kelley could hear the sneer in his voice. Then he slammed the phone down.

'He just wouldn't listen,' Kelley said, turning to Marie. 'Why doesn't he understand?'

'Because he's selfish, that's why,' Marie said. 'Come on, love, don't cry. The worst he can do is write you out of the series. But there'll be other jobs. There must be a clause in your contract for things like this. Have a word with Harry about it.'

They went through to the other room, where Paul was shrugging into his old leather jacket. Although he must have overheard her side of the phone call, he didn't refer to it. 'I'd better be off,' he said. 'But if there's anything I can do, just give me a ring.' He handed her a card. 'Here's my number, just in case you threw the other one away.' Grinning, he got into his car.

As he drove away, Kelley stood in the doorway looking after him. He really was a nice man, she thought, pleased that they were now friends.

14

The next few days passed in a blur of grief and self-recrimination. She should have known her father was ill. But she'd been so wrapped up in her work, as well as her relationship with Carl, that she'd hardly spared him a thought. Now it was too late.

As for the cast and crew of *Land Girls*, they were the last thing on her mind. She wouldn't let herself think about Carl either. Remembering those cruel words, and his total lack of compassion, she wasn't really surprised when he didn't phone again. Why had it taken her so long to see his true nature? However ambitious or dedicated to your business you were, you didn't treat people like that, especially someone you were supposed to be in love with, she thought.

Simon had been more supportive,

although naturally he was concerned about her absence. 'So, when do you think you'll be back?' he asked.

'I'm sorry, Simon, but I really don't know. There's such a lot do. It's not just the funeral. Katy's trying to keep the business running but it'll have to be sold.'

'I understand, pet, but things are getting a bit difficult at this end. We've explained your absence with the tractor accident. At the moment everyone's saying, 'Poor Violet, will she be all right?' And we've got this new girl, Dawn, in hospital covered in bandages. But we can't leave it like that. Violet's such a popular character, and the bandages will have to come off sometime.'

He paused and Kelley could picture him pushing his glasses up his nose. 'I feel terrible letting you down like this, Simon. It's sweet of you to be so understanding.'

'Well, we'll manage — but we do need you back ASAP.'

* * *

After the funeral Marie went back to London, but Kelley had to stay behind. There was so much to sort out. Dad had really let the place go in recent years and there was a lot to do before putting it on the market.

'I've got to see the post office people,' she told Marie on the phone. 'Apparently they were going to close the post office anyway. No wonder Dad was so stressed. It'll take ages to sort things out.'

'What about filming?' Marie said.

'They'd nearly finished anyway. Simon's been great. They've done a re-write with Violet still in hospital but getting better.'

'Will you be in the sequel?' Marie asked.

'Right now I don't care.' Kelley's voice choked on a sob. 'It's so hard. I keep finding bits and pieces of Mum's. Dad didn't get rid of anything.'

'I wish I could be there for you, love.

But we're so busy right now. I'll come down at the weekend.'

★ ★ ★

When Marie arrived on the following Saturday, Kelley was serving in the shop. The post office was closed and Katy Briggs had gone home. The customer left and Marie gave Kelley a hug. 'You look worn out, love. You're working too hard. But the place certainly looks a lot brighter than last time I came.'

'I've got rid of a lot of stuff. Those tins of peas and soup sat on the shelves for ages, getting dusty. I'm concentrating on snacks and drinks and stuff like birthday cards.'

'You're not going to try and keep the business running, I hope.'

'I might.'

When she closed the shop that evening she was exhausted. It was a real pleasure to go through to the kitchen and find that Marie had cooked an appetising meal. For the first time in ages she sat down and ate with enjoyment.

'You're far too skinny, my girl,' Marie chided her. 'And I'll have to do something with your hair. It's growing out and it looks dreadful like that. I'll give you a trim later, then I'll do it properly for you when you come back to London.'

'I'm not coming back, Auntie.'

'But I thought you were going to be in that new series.'

'I haven't heard a thing. No one from the show has bothered to phone. I'm going to stay here and run the shop.'

'You can't do that,' Marie protested. 'This business needs two people to run it. Your dad found that out. No, love, come back to London and stay with me. Get on with your life. You're too young to get stuck in a rut like your dad.'

'I don't really know what to do,' Kelley said.

'Well, it's early days. Why not wait and see if you get a buyer?'

'You're right, Marie. Anyway, I can't put off coming up to town for long. I've got to move the rest of my things out of the flat and give Carl his key. I dread seeing him though.'

'Hasn't he been in touch?'

'No, not a word.'

Marie coloured and looked uncomfortable.

'What's he done?' Kelley asked.

'I didn't want to upset you. You've been through enough already.'

'I'll be more upset if you don't tell me. What is it?'

Marie still hesitated. Then the words came in a rush. 'He's cleared the flat — sent your stuff round to my place.'

'Why didn't he have the decency to phone and ask me to take my things away? He's got this number and my mobile.' She was near to tears.

'Don't cry over him. He's not worth it,' Marie said, her lips set in a grim line. 'That's not all. You're bound to hear. I'm surprised you haven't seen it on the news.'

'I haven't had time to even look at the headlines,' Kelley said.

'Well, that Dawn Fairley's moved in with him. And his wife's had enough. She's divorcing him at last.'

Despite herself, Kelley felt a prickle of pain. All those months when he'd sworn he loved her and would marry her if only he were free. All the secrecy because he didn't want to hurt Angela. He'd soon found someone else *and* everyone knew. What a fool she'd been, and still was. She still missed him, and sometimes the longing to feel his arms around her was almost overwhelming.

She gave herself a mental shake and managed to smile. 'Good luck to the poor girl. She'll need it.' She wasn't sure if her aunt saw through the mask but she was determined to keep it up. She couldn't cope with any more sympathy.

To distract herself, she switched the television on and flicked through the channels. Catching a glimpse of a girl with long fair hair, she quickly switched back to see Dawn Fairley being interviewed.

Kelley turned the sound up and heard her say, 'I'm so lucky to have been given this part so early in my career. It's the big break I was hoping for when I took over from Kelley Robinson in *Land Girls*.'

'I understood Kelley was going to continue as Violet in the new series. But now I hear that she's been written out, killed off. Can you tell us anything about that?' The interviewer sat back, waiting for her answer. Kelley waited too, sitting on the edge of her seat.

'Oh, it's not official yet. You see, poor Kelley's had a lot of problems lately. That's why I had to stand in for her. But I really can't say anything else.'

'But the part you've got in the new series is a similar character to that of Violet, isn't it? In fact, my sources tell me that it is in fact Violet. They've just changed the name.'

'I don't know about that. I just know that I'm looking forward to filming starting in the new year.' Dawn sat back in the chair and looked the interviewer in the eye. Either she was a very good actress or she really didn't know what was going on behind the scenes.

Kelley couldn't watch any more. When Marie came in from the kitchen she was staring at the blank screen, the remote control still in her hand. 'What's the matter, love?'

In a choked voice she said, 'They've killed me off. Dawn Fairley's got my part. How could they do that without letting me know?'

'I don't know, love. Perhaps the silly girl's got it all wrong. Now come on, I promised to do your hair before we went to bed.' She went to her bag and got out her hairdressing scissors. As she got to work she chatted in her cheerful way, trying to take Kelley's mind off the scene she'd witnessed. 'When you come up to town I'll do it properly,' she said. 'If you're determined to go back to your natural colour, I think it would be nice to put some highlights in.'

Kelley looked at herself in the mirror. There were hollows under her eyes and her skin was pale. And Marie was right — she was too thin. Carl's frequent comments had made her self-conscious about her weight and she'd become almost paranoid about getting fat.

With a determined effort she responded to Marie's chatter. When the last lock of blonde hair dropped to the floor Kelley knew that a chapter in her life had really come to an end. From tomorrow she'd start living again, she told herself. Carl was in the past. Her father was gone. It was up to her now to make a new life, perhaps even a new career.

15

It hadn't taken long for Kelley to realise that running a village shop wasn't for her. She'd tried to sell it as a business but there were no offers until it was snapped up by a developer.

She made enough on the sale to buy a small cottage in the Downland village of Rivington. The days were long and lonely and she spent hours walking over the Downs, trying to tire herself out so that she'd sleep at night. And while she walked, she toyed with plans to repay Carl for ruining her career.

Except for Harry and Marie, she had cut herself off from her show-business friends. Harry occasionally sent her news of auditions, but she just wasn't interested.

'Is it because of Roche's threats?' he asked on one of her rare visits to

London. 'Not all directors are frightened of him, you know.'

'It's nothing to do with Carl,' she said.

'But your savings won't last forever,' Harry said.

'I'm working on that,' Kelley told him, but refused to say any more.

When she got back to the cottage, she switched on the laptop. Although acting had lost its appeal, she still wanted to be involved in television and she was working on her second idea. She'd written the outline and opening scene while she was still living in London, but she'd lost the file and had to start from scratch. She must have mislaid the backup in the move, she thought. Marie had assured her that everything stored at her flat had been sent on to the cottage. But it still hadn't turned up and she couldn't waste time looking for it.

When it was finished she printed it out, together with an outline for the following episodes. *Property Ladder* was about a group of friends who bought a dilapidated Victorian house and converted it into flats. With the popularity of makeover and property shows on television, Kelley was confident that her fictional series, with its emphasis on the humorous aspects of doing up old houses, would fill a niche.

But who would take it on now, considering that her reputation among the showbiz set was in tatters?

She decided to ask Simon, although as she listened to his phone ringing, it occurred to her that she didn't know where he was working now. Had he taken up the offer to work in America? She was about to give up when he answered.

'I'm coming up to London today. Can we meet?' she asked.

He seemed pleased to hear from her and suggested lunch at an Italian place not far from Harry's office.

She'd been waiting for ten minutes when he turned up, as dishevelled as ever, peering round the restaurant through his big glasses. She smiled and waved.

'Kelley, pet, I hardly recognised you. What have you been doing to yourself?'

She put a hand to her hair, which still felt a little strange since she'd had it cut short. 'It's the new me,' she said with a laugh.

'Suits you, pet. Now, what did you want to see me about?'

Kelley reached into her shoulder bag and drew out the folder. 'I'd like you to read this. I want your honest opinion. I know I can trust you to tell me what you really think.'

Simon took the folder and opened it, pushing his glasses up his nose. He glanced at the title page, then turned to the treatment she'd written. A waiter approached but he waved the man away, his attention on the manuscript. He read quickly, running his hand through his wiry hair as he turned the pages.

Kelley touched his arm. 'I didn't mean for you to read it straight away. At least let's have lunch first.'

Her smile faded as he looked up, his face serious. 'Where did you get this?' he asked.

'I told you, I wrote it.'

'When?'

'Well, I started it ages ago. When I moved house I lost the backup and had to start over. I've been working on it for ages.' Kelley bit her lip. 'What's wrong, Simon? Have I been wasting my time?'

'No, it's very good. Trouble is — it's not original, is it?'

'What do you mean?' Kelley's heart sank. Had Carl done it again?

Simon looked hard at her. 'You may not have heard, but I've just gone into pre-production on a series that's virtually the same, even down to the title.' He gazed at her earnestly through his big glasses. 'Did you really write this?'

'Of course I did, Simon. I wouldn't lie to you.'

'I'm sorry, pet. This is just too similar to be a coincidence.' He rummaged in his briefcase and brought out a sheaf of papers. 'Look at the opening scene — it's almost word for word.'

Kelley went cold, gripping the edge of the table. His name on the title page told her who was responsible. 'Carl . . .' she gasped.

Simon looked startled. 'Yes, he's producing it. Did you discuss it when you were together?'

'I can assure you we did *not* discuss it. Yes, I started it while I was still with him. But I never spoke to him about this one.' She didn't add that she had kept quiet after suspecting Carl of hijacking her idea for *Going Home*. 'I didn't think anything of it when the memory stick went missing.'

'You're not suggesting Carl stole your work, are you, pet?' Simon bit his lip, looking worried.

'Yes I am. Simon, you must know he's capable of it. I thought I'd deleted it from the laptop, and then I couldn't find the backup. He must have pinched the memory stick when he moved my stuff out of the flat.'

'That's quite an accusation, Kelley.'

She started to protest but Simon interrupted. 'It's not unusual for two people to come up with the same idea. Are you sure you didn't talk to him about it? You were pretty close, after all.'

'I never discussed it with him at all, not after last time.'

'What do you mean?'

'Well, he stole my idea for the follow-up to *Land Girls*.'

'I'm sure that's not true, pet. If Carl hears you spreading stories he'll crucify you. Besides, there's nothing you can do about it. We're just about to start shooting *Property Ladder*.'

'We'll see about that,' Kelley said, gritting her teeth.

Simon looked embarrassed. 'Look, Kelley, we shouldn't be discussing this. I'm committed to working with Carl now. I sympathise, I really do but . . . ' His voice trailed off and he stood up, giving her a quick peck on the cheek.

'It's been nice seeing you, pet. Keep in touch.' Then he was gone.

Kelley stuffed the folder into her bag. 'Spineless wimp,' she muttered through clenched teeth. Anger churned her stomach and she picked up her glass, forcing herself to calm down.

Maybe she couldn't prove anything, but she wouldn't give up. How could she ever have thought she was in love with Carl? she asked herself. She remembered Harry's nickname for him: the Cockroach. And if he were here she'd stamp on him, just like an insect. The thought gave her satisfaction and as she ate her meal, she determined she'd get back at him. She already had an idea about that. But would it work against the rich and powerful Carl Roche?

After lunch she decided to call on Marie. Her aunt would never forgive her if she heard she'd been in London and not been in touch.

Marie welcomed her with a wide smile and the usual bear hug. Clasped to her ample bosom, Kelley felt a wave of love for her. Forcing down the lump in her throat, she recounted her meeting with Simon and was finally able to vent her frustration and anger. Marie listened in silence. Then she patted Kelley's hand. 'We'll discuss it with Harry. He'll be here later. He'll know what to do.'

Harry was sympathetic but, like Simon, he thought it unlikely they could prove Carl had stolen her script. Unless he used it word for word, he only had to make a few changes to the characters and locations to get away with it.

'How can I be sure it won't happen again?' Kelley wailed.

'If you sent any future scripts to one of the big production companies, you'd be safe enough. There aren't many around like the Cockroach, thank God,' Harry said.

'Why don't we ask Paul's advice?' Marie said. 'He's a writer — he'll know about copyright.'

'I'd rather not. Next thing you know I'll be reading about it in the paper.'

'Don't be silly. He's a nice bloke, despite being a journalist,' Marie said.

'I thought Simon was a nice bloke too. And a friend. Yet he took Carl's side straight away.'

'Look at it from Simon's point of view, love. He's not in a position to cross Carl. That American offer fell through and this is the only job he could get. And he could lose that if Carl found out you'd talked to him,' Marie said.

Harry finished eating and laid his knife and fork down. 'Why don't I speak to Paul? He needn't know it's anything to do with Kelley.'

He went into the living room to use the phone while Kelley and Marie cleared the table. When he came back he looked solemn. 'We were right. We can't prove anything without the backup. He's sorry he can't help this time.'

'You didn't tell him it was me?'

'No, I told him it was a writer friend but he guessed. He's quite concerned about you.'

'There, I told you he was a nice young man,' Marie said with a fond smile.

'It's a story he wants, that's all,' Kelley said.

Harry changed the subject. 'You're not giving up acting altogether, are you? I'm still trying for auditions, you know.'

'Trying! Well, obviously you've been unsuccessful. I wonder why?'

'It's Roche,' Marie said. 'He's been spreading stories about you.'

'I knew it. What's he been saying?'

Harry gave an embarrassed cough. 'It seems that you're 'difficult' to work with — unreliable — rumours of drugs, drinking.'

'Perhaps I'd better stick to writing then — that's if he doesn't mess that up too.' Kelley was furious but, determined not to be beaten by Carl Roche, she said good night and hurried to catch the last train. She couldn't wait to get home and start working on her plan.

16

It was a beautiful day and Kelley took her coffee and her laptop into the garden. The grass needed cutting and the roses were crying out for dead-heading, but she didn't spare them a glance.

As she typed furiously, a cool breeze sprung up and she rubbed her bare arms. But she scarcely felt the cold, her mind busy with her plan to make Carl pay for what he'd done to her. Writing a new series was just the first step.

When she'd finished the outline and first episode of the story, she made two backup copies. One she put in a padded envelope with a note to Harry asking him to keep it in his safe. She'd send it recorded delivery in the morning and make sure she put the posting slip somewhere safe. She wasn't taking any chances this time. The other went into her handbag.

She switched the laptop off and leaned back with a sigh, massaging the back of her neck. It was the best thing she'd done yet. Now for the next step.

Given that her reputation in show business had been ruined, Kelley realised how hard it would be to get a producer interested in the series. The solution, she had decided, was to start up her own production company, and that would take money — more than she could afford. She'd need a backer, someone who believed in her enough to invest their money. She couldn't do it on her own.

Surely Marie and Harry would help, she told herself, getting up and stretching, stiff after hours spent on the laptop. But could she tell them the whole story? She wasn't even sure she could go through with it. A lot of her anger had dispersed over the past few months as she'd thrown herself into her writing. Maybe getting revenge wasn't such a good idea. Then she remembered the others who'd been hurt by

Carl's cruel arrogance, and the misuse of the power his position had given him.

With a sigh, she made up her mind. There was someone she must see before she could put the plan into practice.

She grabbed her jacket and handbag and drove the few miles to Lydford, parking in the driveway of the Old Rectory. Taking a deep breath, she knocked on the door. Her courage almost failed her when Angela Roche opened it.

'What are you doing here?' she asked in a cool, clipped voice.

Kelley stood her ground. 'Give me five minutes — please.'

The woman hesitated, eyes narrowed as she looked Kelley over from top to toe. 'I can't imagine what you could have to say to me.'

Kelley chose her words carefully. 'I hate to sound impertinent, but would you mind telling me what your relationship with Carl is at the moment?'

'You've got a nerve, young lady, considering you were partly to blame for the break-up of my marriage.' For a moment Angela's coolness appeared to have deserted her and her blue eyes flashed fire.

Kelley's heart sank. Angela obviously believed the sleazy stories that were circulating about her. She didn't blame Angela. And, although she'd tried to tell herself her relationship with Carl was different, when all was said and done she had had an affair with him. Perhaps she'd been too optimistic, hoping Angela would help. She shrugged. 'I'm sorry. I shouldn't have come.' She turned away.

'Wait. You can't go without telling me what this is all about. Come in and have a cup of coffee. You've aroused my curiosity.'

Kelley was shown into the drawing room, where she sat on the edge of the sofa, wishing that she hadn't come.

Angela came in carrying a loaded tray. She poured the coffee, handed

Kelley a cup and sat down opposite her. 'Now, perhaps you'll be good enough to tell me why you're here.'

Kelley swallowed. 'I'm sorry. I had the stupid idea that you might help me. I haven't been thinking straight lately.'

Angela lit a cigarette and squinted at Kelley through the smoke, an amused glint in her eye. 'Why should my husband's mistress come to me for help? Sorry, perhaps I should say ex-mistress. I gather he's dumped you for someone else.'

'That's not true. I left him,' Kelley said, her face flaming. 'I suppose he had to say that to save face,' she added, her chin up defiantly.

'You're not still in love with him, are you?' Angela's voice had softened.

'I hate him.'

'Join the club,' Angela said sharply. 'He's done this once too often. I've had enough. That's why I'm divorcing him and stinging him for every penny I can get. Now, how can I help?'

'I want to get even with him.' Kelley

put down her coffee cup and told her story, her voice gaining in confidence. 'He stole my script — not once but twice. And there was nothing I could do about it,' she concluded bitterly.

'But you've thought of a way to get even?' Angela asked.

'Perhaps. With your help,' Kelley said.

Angela nodded approval, a smile twisting her lips as Kelley outlined her plan. 'This beats making a bonfire of his Armani suits or giving all his champagne away,' she said with a laugh.

Kelley laughed with her. 'Don't get me wrong. If it was just a broken romance, I'd crawl away and try to get over it. But he cheated me. I can't prove a thing and he got away with it. But if you agree to help, he'll be discredited and maybe it will stop him doing it again.'

'I think it's a marvellous idea. And he'll fall for it. He's greedy — not just for money, but for fame and success. He won't be able to stop himself,' Angela said.

'Can we make it work?' Kelley asked.

'Carl sometimes worked at home — not that he was here often. He moved most of his bits and pieces out a few weeks ago.' She stood up. 'Come on, I'll show you.'

They walked down the hall to Carl's study. A desk stood under the window and empty shelves lined the walls. A cardboard box full of floppy disks, CDs, USB drives and cables stood in a corner. 'He said he'll pick up the rest of his things later,' Angela said.

Kelley took the memory stick out of her bag and handed it to her new ally. Angela smiled and dropped it into the box.

'Let's hope he doesn't sort his stuff out too soon,' Kelley said. 'I've got to get the other part organised yet.'

Angela invited Kelley to stay for lunch and, as they chatted over the meal, Kelley found herself warming to the other woman. For the first time she found herself able to talk openly about her relationship with Carl.

'I really loved him. And I wanted to make him happy. When he lost his temper and got violent I always thought it was my fault — if I hadn't upset him . . . ' Kelley faltered and Angela nodded sympathetically.

'You're a brave girl, Kelley,' she said. 'You faced up to what he was doing to you and had the sense to get out. We haven't all got your strength. But there comes a time when you have to say enough is enough.'

'Well, you got there in the end,' Kelley said.

As they parted after lunch, Angela said, 'I'll let you know if he collects his stuff.'

'Thank you. I'll keep in touch.'

★   ★   ★

Now that she was sure of Angela's help, Kelley couldn't wait to get started. And for that she needed Harry and Marie, the only two people in the world she loved and trusted. They would help with setting up her business. But would they connive at setting Carl up too?

She phoned Harry and arranged to meet at the salon. The next day she caught the early train to London, carrying a folder containing her business plan. It wasn't just that she wanted to get even with Carl, she told herself. She was excited at the prospect of trying something new.

Her main worry was that, even if they agreed to help, Marie and Harry stood to lose money if she failed. Was it really fair to expect them to risk so much for her? But although there was some left from the sale of her father's business, it wasn't enough. She needed investment.

They can only say no, she thought as she hurried to find a taxi.

Marie was with a client but when Harry arrived she joined them upstairs and the three of them sat down to discuss Kelley's proposal. When she'd finished her pitch, neither of them spoke for a few moments.

She thought they were going to turn

her down until Harry's face split in a wide grin. Marie still looked uncertain. 'I'm quite happy to invest money in your venture, love. But I don't see how starting your own company is going to destroy Carl,' she said.

'Don't you see, Marie? I start producing my own show but we swear everyone to secrecy. When Angela gives Carl his stuff, he's bound to find the memory stick with my script on it. He thinks he's got another ready-made programme that he can claim is all his own work, just like he did with my other two. But I can prove it's mine because Harry will have the other backup in his safe.'

'Have you got it with you?' Harry asked.

'I posted it before I got the train. That way it'll have a postmark, as well as me having the recorded delivery slip. And I know your secretary books in your mail with a date and time of receipt.'

'Good thinking,' Harry said.

Marie still looked puzzled. 'How do you know he'll use it?'

'I don't think he'll be able to resist it. But it doesn't matter if he doesn't. I'll still have my own company, producing my own programmes. But if he is tempted, I'll challenge him. I'll have already started work on my show so we'll have him cold.' Kelley sat back with a triumphant grin.

Harry chimed in, 'And, even if it never gets as far as a court case, the mud will stick. There's a lot of people in the business who would like to see the arrogant swine get his come-uppance.'

'It's all a bit complicated for me, love,' Marie said. 'But if you think it'll work, I'm game.'

'Thanks, Marie. But I'm worried about you losing money if things go wrong.'

'I can afford it,' Marie said with a smile.

'So can I — and it'll be worth every penny,' Harry agreed.

'Suppose Carl hears what we're up to,' Kelley said. 'He hasn't forgiven me for being the one to dump him. I don't think anyone's ever had the guts to walk out on him before. And he can be very vindictive.'

'But he won't know it's you, will he? You'll be using a different name,' Marie said.

'I'm just worried about the press getting hold of the story before we're ready.'

'Why don't we have a test run?' Harry suggested. 'We'll go to Patti's and introduce you as Joanne Kelley. I bet no one will recognise you, but even if they do it won't matter. We'll just have to think of another way to get at the Cockroach.'

17

A few weeks later Kelley was sitting alone in Patti's. It was her first appearance in public since the demise of Violet, as well as her debut appearance as Joanne Kelley of Kelley's Eye Productions.

She was ready now to face Carl and his new lover. She knew he'd be there tonight. He was celebrating his birthday as he always did, with a lavish meal and flowing champagne.

She would be celebrating, too, when Harry and Marie arrived. Harry had found premises in Holton which were ideal for a television studio. A local builder had jumped at the chance of doing the conversion and the work was going well. In a few months she'd be ready to start filming *Nore Bay* — the series she hoped would bring about Carl's downfall.

If she were honest, she had to admit that vengeance was no longer such a burning desire. Harry and Marie's enthusiasm for the project had given her confidence in its success. Beating Carl at his own game should be revenge enough. But she still longed to see him squirm.

But he mustn't find out who was behind Kelley's Eye Productions. If she came face-to-face with him tonight and he didn't recognise her, and she could be confident that he wouldn't connect her with it, he'd be less likely to try and sabotage it. Still, she'd have to be careful. Carl was a dangerous enemy.

When he came in with Dawn Fairley on his arm, followed by a crowd of hangers-on, Kelley's anger burned anew. As his gaze swept over her without even a glimmer of recognition, fury boiled up and she wanted to throw the contents of her glass in his face. She watched him drinking in the fawning admiration of his hangers-on and knew that she wouldn't be satisfied until she'd seen him brought down.

She was still simmering when the lights went out and the waiter brought the birthday cake in. How she wished she had the courage to get up and confront him in front of his cronies. Fortunately Harry and Marie arrived and she calmed down.

Harry insisted on ordering champagne to celebrate the launch of Kelley's Eye and to her surprise, as the evening went on, she almost managed to forget Carl's presence.

Then Paul came in with Mick Gamble. They stopped by their table and Paul asked Harry what they were celebrating. Kelley held her breath. If Paul found out that she was behind Kelley's Eye, it would be in the papers tomorrow. But her new hairdo and the soft restaurant lighting meant that he might not realise it was her. All the same, she bent down, fumbling with her shoe until they moved away. He hadn't noticed her but, feeling shaky, she asked to leave as soon as they'd finished their meal.

Paul had been trying to contact Kelley for weeks. He tried to kid himself he was only after a story, but he had to admit it was her he was interested in. He'd even been down to Holton Regis and inquired at the old post office shop, but it was closed and awaiting development.

He'd returned to London, determined to tackle Marie again. She was only trying to protect Kelley, but he had to convince her that he really cared for her. But Marie fobbed him off.

He joined Mick, making notes as the camera flashed, but his heart wasn't in it. He glanced back at the table where Marie and her party sat. Where was Kelley now? he wondered.

It took a while before the penny dropped. That girl sitting with them — was it her? He hadn't noticed her at first. She'd changed since he'd last seen her after her father's death. He pushed his way between the crowded tables, just as they stood up to leave. By the time he reached the door, their taxi was pulling away.

Mick, noticing his frantic dash for the exit, caught up with him, camera at the ready. 'Who was that? Anyone interesting?' His paparazzi antennae were quivering and he was almost panting, like a dog scenting a fox.

Paul struggled to hide his contempt. 'No one you'd be interested in. I thought I spotted an old friend, that's all.' Mick's shoulders slumped, disappointed, and he lowered the camera.

Paul, sensing the photographer's thoughts, wondered if people saw him like that. He hoped not. He'd always tried to keep his integrity. He'd have to get out of this game, he thought, as he said goodnight to his companion and went back to his flat, still thinking of Kelley.

Being on the spot when she got the news of her father's illness had strengthened their friendship — but it wasn't just friendship he wanted. It hadn't been the right time to reveal his feelings, especially given her dislike of journalists. He didn't really blame her for not trusting the press — or him.

But from what he knew of her, she wasn't the sort to run away and hide. What was she up to? Whatever it was, he was sure that both he and showbiz hadn't heard the last of Kelley Robinson.

Perhaps he'd ask Harry to arrange an interview — purely professional interest, of course. He knew the rumours of drugs and drink were untrue. Maybe she'd let him be the one to set the record straight.

18

Harry had gone to his office and Marie was downstairs in the salon. Alone in the flat, Kelley sat at the dining table with papers spread round her, chewing the end of her pen and wondering if she'd taken on too much. There seemed to be so much more involved in setting up the studio than she'd anticipated.

She was anxious to get back to Sussex to oversee the building work. It was going well and she hoped they'd be ready to start filming the new series in the spring. But there was still a lot of planning to do and she'd decided to stay in London for a few more days to get the paperwork sorted. At least with Marie and Harry's investment in the business, finance wasn't a problem.

The buzzer sounded from downstairs and she jumped up. Harry must have forgotten his key, she thought. She pressed the switch to release the downstairs door and called out to him to come up. But when she opened the door she almost closed it again.

Before she could speak, Paul said, 'It *is* you. I almost didn't recognise you last night. Why didn't you speak to me?'

Kelley didn't know what to say. Part of her was pleased to see him, but if he found out what she doing, it could spoil everything. 'Paul, I . . . '

'I know you don't trust me,' he said. 'But please talk to me.'

Kelley stepped back and opened the door wider. 'You'd better come in,' she said in a resigned voice, leading him through to the sitting room. 'Can I get you a drink or anything?'

'No thank you.' Paul walked to the window and looked out at the busy street.

'I suppose you're here for a story.' Kelley said bitterly.

Paul turned to face her. 'No, I've been worried about you. You must believe that I had nothing to do with

211

those newspaper stories. I think you've been treated badly. If I wrote anything at all it would be to set the record straight.'

Kelley found herself softening at the undoubted sincerity in his voice. 'Do you really mean that?' she asked.

'I don't lie,' he said indignantly.

She apologised, then made a decision. 'Sit down and I'll tell you all about it — on one condition.'

'That I don't print anything, right?' Paul took her hand and said earnestly. 'I promise — strictly off the record. I wouldn't do anything to hurt you, Kelley.'

He listened silently as she told him why she and Carl had split up and what she'd been doing since she left *Land Girls*.

'I never believed what they said about you breaking your contract. When your father died, Marie told me they were keeping the part open for you until you were able to come back.'

'That's what I thought,' Kelley said

bitterly. 'I only found out I'd been killed off when the episode aired. I couldn't believe it and phoned Simon the next day. He said Carl had told him I wasn't coming back. And it was too late by then . . . '

'I had a feeling Roche was behind it.'

'He said I'd let them down. We had a big row. But I'd already decided to leave him before my father died.'

'Do you regret it?' Paul asked softly.

'Definitely not. I'm just glad I had the courage to do it. The worst thing is that he seems to have it in for me now.'

'He can't bear being crossed. I suspect he can't forgive you for dumping him.'

'Yes — but he found someone else soon enough, didn't he? In fact I wouldn't be surprised if he was seeing Dawn while I was still with him.' Kelley was pleased that finally she was able to admit that without pain.

'You hurt his pride. And he has to be in control, you know that,' Paul said. 'Still, it's a shame he stopped you working on the sequel. For someone who rates success so highly, it was rather short-sighted of him. Dawn Fairley's not a patch on you and, although *Going Home* isn't a bad series, it's not as good as it could be.'

'Serves him right. He shouldn't have pinched my script and tried to pass it off as his own work.' Kelley paused. 'I think I could have forgiven that. He sounded so reasonable when I tackled him about it. But then he did it again.'

'What do you mean?' Paul asked.

'I wrote a treatment and first episode for another series. I'm sure he took the memory stick with it on. I couldn't believe it when Simon Kent told me he was already working on the same series for Carl. He'd even given it the same title — *Property Ladder*.'

'The rat. How did he get away with it?'

'Harry investigated but I hadn't protected my copyright. I didn't even realise I had to.' Kelley sighed. 'So, he got away with it again.'

'Did you threaten to sue him?'

'Harry advised me not to — Carl has already done enough damage to my career.'

Paul nodded agreement. 'He's ruined a lot of people who've crossed him.' He got up and paced the room. 'You know, he tried to bribe me once to put something in the paper about someone. When I refused he resorted to threats and blackmail.' He gave a short laugh. 'Luckily I haven't got any dark secrets in my past so I called his bluff. He still hates me.'

'He was furious when he found out I'd let you interview me,' Kelley told him.

'No wonder you were suspicious of me. He must have planted the idea in your mind that I wasn't to be trusted.'

Kelley smiled. 'I'm sorry. I should've known better. I should have listened to Marie. She's a very good judge of character.' She patted the sofa beside her. 'Come and sit down and I'll tell you a bit more about my new project.

But I warn you, I'm not ready to go public yet.'

Paul put his hand on his heart and gave a wry grin. 'You can trust me,' he said. They laughed together as he sat beside her and Kelley felt as if a load had been lifted off her.

* * *

Later, as she let Paul out of the flat with the promise to keep in touch, she wondered why she hadn't told him about the plan she had hatched with Angela. She told herself she couldn't risk Carl finding out. But in her heart she knew that she couldn't bear the thought of Paul's disapproval. She had warmed to him from their very first meeting, and despite her reservations about the way he earned his living, she had always liked him. Their meeting today had strengthened her liking and she found herself looking forward to seeing him again.

When Harry returned she was deep

in paperwork and she didn't mention Paul's visit. They worked together for the rest of the afternoon, using her laptop to make spreadsheets of what needed to be done, and tossing ideas back and forth to each other.

Harry leaned back in his chair, throwing down the pencil he'd been playing with. He took his glasses off and rubbed his eyes. 'I think that's it for now. We can't do anything else until the building's ready.'

Marie came in as they were finishing up. 'You look like you could do with a drink, love,' she said, going to the sideboard and pouring whisky into a glass. 'What about you, Kelley?'

Kelley shook her head, stood up and stretched. 'I'd rather have a nice long soak in the bath.'

'How's it going then?' Marie said.

'Great,' Harry said. 'This young lady seems to have quite a flair for business. She's come up with some great ideas. We'll start getting a team together soon.'

'Don't forget, they mustn't know who they're working for. I won't let Carl sabotage this project, and he'll try if he finds out it's me, I just know it,' Kelley said.

'Stop worrying, girl. It'll be OK,' Harry said with a reassuring grin. 'Why don't we all go out for a meal and forget business for a while.'

Marie laughed. 'Since when did you want to forget about business? You know you're enjoying this.'

'I must admit I like the challenge of doing something different. The old firm can run itself for a while until we get this off the ground.' He took his jacket off the back of the chair. 'Come on, girls. Go and get ready. I'll phone for a table.'

19

Harry and Kelley were in Holton, checking up on the conversion of the warehouse.

'Going well, Kelley,' Harry said. 'Time to see about ordering the equipment. Meanwhile we'd better let these lads get on with the work.'

They had lunch at a pub on the seafront and, as they ate, Harry talked enthusiastically about the project. Kelley had been worried that he and Marie had only helped out of affection for her. But she realised he was really enjoying the challenge. His enthusiasm helped boost her confidence; she'd sometimes felt a little overwhelmed by the enormity of what she'd taken on.

'I'm not bothered about the practical side — the building work, buying the equipment, all that,' Harry said, waving his fork about. 'But we must have a good production team, especially the director.'

'Who do you suggest?' Kelley asked.

'Why not ask Simon?'

Kelley remembered her last meeting with him. 'No,' she declared adamantly. 'He's too loyal to Carl. Well, scared of him, more like.' She almost spat the words, recalling how hurt she'd been when her so-called friends had deserted her.

'It's worth a try though. You've worked with him before and you admire his work. I can't think of a better person. Why not ask him?'

'You ask him, Harry. But I don't expect him to agree,' Kelley said, pushing her half-eaten dessert away.

'You can't let personal feelings enter into it if you want to be successful. He's the best and I'm going to try and persuade him.'

Harry went to the bar to order coffee and while he was gone Kelley thought over what he'd said.

When he came back with the drinks,

she covered his hand with hers. 'You're right as usual. But it's no good. Simon's already committed to Carl on his new series — my series I should say.'

'You never know. He might be free by the time we're ready to start shooting.'

Kelley still had reservations. Even if Simon agreed, she still felt awkward about encountering the people she'd worked with in her previous life. But she couldn't hide forever, especially as she still intended to be involved in the close-knit world of television. She smiled at Harry. 'I'll leave the hiring and firing to you. After all, you're the one with the contacts.'

After lunch they walked back along the windswept promenade to where Harry had parked the car.

He drove her back to Rivington and dropped her at the cottage, where she threw open the windows, letting the cold air in. The place needed airing after being shut up for a week. Keeping her coat on, she went through the kitchen and put the kettle on.

She took her coffee to the desk and switched on the computer. But she sat there letting her coffee grow cold, her mind as blank as the screen. What was she thinking of? How could she, an inexperienced actress, hope to produce and direct a show that would topple the great Carl Roche from his place at the top? What was more, how dare she contemplate tricking the man whose power and deviousness were feared by so many?

But she had Marie and Harry behind her, as well as Angela. There must be others willing to stand up to him — maybe even Simon.

With that thought she set to work with new determination. A couple of hours later she was interrupted by Harry on the phone.

'I've spoken to Simon. And he's interested. We're meeting at my office next week.'

'He doesn't know it's me, does he?' Kelley asked.

'I just told him I was setting up a

production company with a friend and needed a director.'

'What about the series he's doing?'

'It's all off. When they went into pre-production on the new show, Carl wanted too much control. So Simon opted out. I'll tell you about it when you come up to town next week.'

'At least he's finally had the guts to stand up to Carl. Maybe he'll believe now that he really did steal my script.'

'I hope you won't try to embroil him in your little plot,' Harry said.

'Of course not. I wish now I hadn't involved you and Marie. I'm beginning to have second thoughts.'

'It's up to you, love. Nothing's too bad for the Cockroach. But there's still time to back out if you've got cold feet.'

'I'll think about it,' Kelley said, putting the phone down. Perhaps she was wrong to try and get back at Carl. It wasn't in her nature to be vindictive. But then, no one had ever hurt her the way Carl had.

Later, after completing several more

pages of her script, Kelley switched off the machine and sat back feeling much more optimistic about the future than she had earlier in the day.

She made a sandwich and switched the television on. *TV World* was showing — and there was Carl, talking about his new series. *My* new series, she thought angrily, turning the sound up.

'Let's hear what the Cockroach has to say,' she muttered through clenched teeth.

He was wearing his media face, all candid blue eyes and even white teeth. Kelley was so busy hating him she almost missed it. But she, who knew him so well, noticed the minute change in his expression, the fractional hardening of the eyes. When he ran his fingers through his hair, clasped his hands between his knees and leaned forward, Kelley knew it was a pose.

'Simon Kent has worked with me on a number of projects,' he said. 'I admire his work tremendously. It's unfortunate that prior commitments prevent him working with me again on this new show.'

'Then it's not true that he walked out after a difference of opinion?' the interviewer said.

'As I said, Simon had prior commitments.' Carl leaned back in his chair with an expression that said he wasn't prepared to discuss it further.

'Would you work with him in future?' the interviewer persisted. It was common knowledge that when Carl fell out with someone, they never worked with him again — in fact were lucky to find work anywhere.

'I don't see why not,' Carl replied with a smile. If Kelley hadn't known better, she'd have sworn he was sincere. It was easy to see why he remained such a popular figure with the public.

As she switched off she remembered that *TV World* was one of Carl's own programmes and he'd once been its presenter. She realised that he'd known what questions would be asked. He'd probably written the script beforehand. So much for live television.

Why couldn't people see it, she thought, marvelling at his continuing popularity. Then she answered her own question. She'd had to live with him before she realised what he was really like. She too had been taken in by his easy charm.

She paced the room, furious with him, but more so with herself for being taken in by him — angry most of all that he still had the power to stir her emotions, even negative ones. Why did she let him do it? Why couldn't she just forget him and get on with her life? She took a deep breath, willing herself to calm down.

She couldn't go through life not switching on the television or picking up a newspaper in case she saw his hated face. In the small world of entertainment she'd have to come face to face with him some time. When that day came, she vowed she would not let him intimidate her.

The surge of anger fuelled her determination to get even with the Cockroach. She *would* go ahead with her plan. Her earlier doubts driven away, she prepared for bed and slept well, waking refreshed and ready to get on with her life.

When Paul phoned to ask how things were going, she was really pleased to hear his voice.

'Are you sure this is off the record?' she asked with a teasing laugh.

'Of course it is.' Paul's voice was indignant.

'I'm sorry, just joking,' Kelley said. 'The builders are getting on with the studio. It should be finished on schedule. And Harry's started inter-viewing and auditioning.'

'I'll have to come down some time and have a look round.'

'That'd be great, but I won't be there for a few days. I've got a meeting in London with Harry on Tuesday.'

'Perhaps we can meet up then?'

Kelley hesitated. She still wasn't sure of his motives, but she had to believe his promises that he wouldn't write anything till she was ready. 'I'll give you a ring,' she said.

20

On the train to Victoria, Kelley was lost in thought. She looked out of the window, noticing that the trees were starting to bud and a few early daffodils bloomed in sheltered spots along the embankment. It reminded her that they were due to start filming soon. She'd told Paul she'd give him the story when they were ready to start. Was that why he wanted to see her? Did he only want to pump her for information?

But she couldn't believe that. She was beginning to like him a lot and she hoped she'd see him while she was in town. She got out her mobile and left a message saying she'd be calling at Marie's later on.

The train pulled into Victoria and with an effort, she dismissed thoughts of Paul as she picked up her bags and hurried to find a taxi. She must concentrate on her meeting.

Outside Harry's office she felt a churning in her stomach. Would Simon be there already, and would he pull out once he realised who was producing the show?

Harry got up from his desk and gave her a hug. 'You're looking lovely, sweetheart. The country air must be good for you. Come and sit down.' He turned to the man by the window. 'Simon, Kelley's here.'

His eyes widened and, after a brief pause, his face creased in a grin. 'Oh, I get it — Kelley's Eye.'

Kelley stifled the urge to giggle at his expression as he said, 'You've really set up your own business? Does Carl know?'

'It's none of his business.'

'You're right,' Simon said, his mouth set in a grim line.

'Well, we're not here to talk about him,' Kelley said. 'Harry's already told you about the new company. We'll be ready to start filming soon and we need a director. I hope it will be you.'

Simon, still smiling in a rather bemused way, pushed his glasses up his nose, oblivious to the fact that they slipped down again. 'I can't get over it. We all thought you'd dropped out of the business.'

'I've been keeping a low profile. For the moment, it's best no one knows I'm behind Kelley's Eye. I'm sure you understand why.'

'Carl's still furious with you. We all knew he was behind the rumours.'

'Well, if anyone asks, you must say the boss of Kelley's Eye is Joanne Kelley — Joanne was my mother's name.'

Simon pushed his glasses up again, looking embarrassed, cleared his throat and said in a rush, 'Kelley, pet, I had nothing to do with all this. I didn't know what to say when you came to see me about your script. You do under-stand, don't you?'

'Yes. But there's something you have to understand. I didn't just walk out. It was a huge shock, hearing by chance that Violet had been killed off. And when I tried to get more acting work no one would hire me because they thought I was unreliable.' Kelley coughed to hide the lump in her throat.

'Of course you had to go home when your father died. We've had to juggle with scripts before through illness and suchlike. I didn't understand Carl's reaction, especially as you two were so close . . .'

'It's true, we were having an affair, but I'm over it now. He was furious with me because I walked out on *him*, not the show. That's why he's been so vindictive.'

Simon nodded thoughtfully. While they'd been talking Harry had poured the coffee and set out papers on the table. He turned to Simon and said, 'Well, now that we've got that out of the way — are you in?'

'I can't wait to get started.' Simon grinned. 'If Kelley's script is anywhere near as good as the one Carl stole, we'll be on to a winner.' He turned to her with an apologetic shrug. 'I know *Going Home* was your idea but Carl wouldn't hear of having your name anywhere on the credits. And *Property Ladder*, the one you asked me about, was just as good. In a way I wish I was directing, but Carl's become impossible to work with.'

'Do you believe me now? It *was* my script. Carl stole it, just as he did the sequel to *Land Girls*. Oh, he changed it a bit, but it was mine — only I couldn't prove it.'

'Well, he won't get a chance. We'll keep it under wraps,' Simon said, picking up the folder. 'Now let's get down to business.'

There was a few minutes' silence as he read. 'Good idea . . . different,' he muttered, stacking the pages together. 'This'll knock spots off anything Roche has in the pipeline,' he said. 'That is the idea isn't it, to beat him at his own game?'

Kelley nodded, although she couldn't

tell him at this stage that this was only part of the plan. She got up and hugged him. 'You really like it?' she said.

'Yes, I do. Now, we'll need a cameraman, and lighting people.' He got up and paced the floor, waving his arms and pushing his glasses up as the ideas flowed.

Kelley clutched Harry's hand. It was all right. She was going to produce her own show. And it would be a success. As Simon talked, she scribbled in her notebook and the coffee grew cold.

'Well, that's it for now. Let me know when the equipment arrives and we can get started,' Simon said, shaking Harry's hand and giving Kelley a hug.

When he'd gone Harry looked at his watch. 'I told Marie I'd pick her up. We're taking you out tonight.'

Traffic was building up and Harry tapped the wheel impatiently but it was early evening by the time they pulled up outside the salon. Kelley leapt out of the car and rushed upstairs.

'Marie, we're all set. Simon's direct-ing — he's really keen.' She stopped short as she spotted Paul. So, he'd got her message. Although she'd hoped to run into him, she wasn't quite sure how she felt now seeing him there, looking quite at home in her aunt's flat.

He grinned. 'Hi, Kelley. Marie's asked me to join you all for a meal,' he said.

Kelley glanced at Marie, who gave a sly smile. 'I knew you wouldn't mind,' she said.

'Of course not. I'd better get changed.' She rushed upstairs, feeling a little confused. But as she changed out of her jeans and sweater into a simple dress of jade green with a matching jacket, she had to admit she'd been pleased to see him. She brushed her short brown hair so that it framed her face, the golden highlights forming a shining halo, and glanced in the mirror. No one would recognise her as the naive young woman who'd played Violet.

21

They went to Patti's of course, although Kelley would have preferred somewhere quieter. Harry as usual was in great form, laughing and toasting Kelley's success. 'To the downfall of the Cockroach,' he declaimed, draining his glass and setting it down with a flourish.

'I'll drink to that,' Marie agreed.

But Kelley was silent. She hadn't given Carl a thought for weeks. Suddenly she remembered her deal with Angela. But now that everything was going so well, the idea of revenge seemed petty. Surely it should be enough just to prove she could make it on her own. She wondered whether Angela felt the same way or if her desire for vengeance still burned as brightly. She'd have to speak to her soon and find out.

She leaned across and whispered to Harry, 'Not so loud, please. I don't want anyone to know . . . ' She didn't want to remind Harry that one of the reasons for secrecy was her plan to trick Carl into stealing her script. Just lately, she'd been on the verge of giving up the scheme to discredit him. And besides, now that she was becoming so fond of Paul, she didn't want him to find out. She couldn't bear him to think badly of her.

'All right, sweetheart. I'll keep mum,' Harry said, winking at her.

She glanced at Paul, hoping he wouldn't ask what they meant. 'You'll have your story soon,' she promised.

'Whenever you're ready,' he said, taking her hand. 'I understand why you want to keep quiet for the moment.'

They had resumed their meal when Carl swept in, silencing the buzz of conversation and dominating the room with his presence. Dawn Fairley was with him and Kelley couldn't help comparing the tall, slim blonde with her own understated looks.

But why should she care? Paul squeezed her hand and she returned the pressure. Carl stroked Dawn's hair, seemingly oblivious to their dinner companions, and Kelley realised she felt nothing at all for the man she'd once thought she loved. Even the burning hatred had gone. He wasn't worth the effort, she thought, at the same time wondering how she could have been taken in by him.

Marie was watching her anxiously. 'We can leave if you like,' she whispered. 'But don't let him upset you, love.'

'It's OK. He doesn't bother me,' Kelley said, surprising herself with the truth of the statement. She smiled and stood up. 'Back in a minute,' she said.

Threading her way through the tables to the door at the rear of the restaurant, she passed close to Carl's table. He looked up and stared straight at her. She saw his eyes widen as he recognised her. Calling upon all her acting skills, she summoned up a brittle smile. 'Hello, Carl. How are you?' she said.

His eyes narrowed and she knew that if he realised what she was up to, he would try to sabotage her new venture. 'I'm well,' he said. 'What about you? Haven't seen you on the box lately. Resting, are we?' His smile was as cold as his eyes.

She didn't answer and swept past him. In the rest room, she leaned on the washbasin, her breath coming in short gasps. During their months together he'd often frightened her, although his attacks had never been really physical. She looked at herself in the mirror — face pale, eyes wide. She wouldn't let him get to her, she vowed, splashing her face with cold water.

As she repaired her makeup, the door opened and someone rushed into the lavatory, slamming the door. The stifled sob effectively diverted her attention from her own feelings and she called, 'Are you all right?' Silly question, she thought. 'Can I do anything to help?'

'No. Leave me alone. I'll be OK in a minute.' The voice was Dawn's. What had Carl done now? She turned the taps on and washed her hands, leaving the water running to mask the sound of crying and holding her hands under the roar of hot air for much longer than necessary. She heard the bolt drawn back, and Dawn emerged, mascara streaked, lipstick smudged. Kelley met the other girl's eyes in the mirror above the washbasin.

'OK now?' she asked.

Dawn nodded mutely and another tear ran down her face. Kelley put her arm round the girl's shoulders. 'Want to tell me about it?'

'He can be such a pig sometimes.' Kelley nodded silent agreement and Dawn went on. 'He was laughing about you. How he ditched you and stopped you getting work. Someone at our table told him they'd heard you were producing a new series. He got really nasty; said no-one walks out on him and gets away with it.'

Dawn's eyes sparked with anger. She went to the mirror and began repairing her makeup. Kelley leaned against the washbasin and watched her. 'Go on, what else did he say?'

'I thought he was upset because you'd broken up. I gave him a kiss and said not to worry, he's still got me.' Dawn bit her lip, trying to control herself. But there was a quiver in her voice as she went on. 'He pushed me away and said, 'Only as long as I want you.' He said I was just an ornament.' Dawn burst into tears again.

'You don't have to put up with it, Dawn,' Kelley said. 'He needs people like us to boost his ego. I really thought I loved him. Even when I discovered what he was really like I made excuses, forgave him. But there comes a time when you have to say enough's enough.'

'I'm not like you, Kelley. I can't speak up for myself.' Dawn sniffed and wiped her eyes. 'Besides, he's promised me a part in his new show. I get to wear the most fabulous dresses.' She smiled as she applied her lipstick, but her hand was trembling.

Kelley sighed. Was Dawn really as shallow as she appeared? But despite her exasperation, she understood. 'Dawn, if you ever need a friend . . . '

But Dawn carried on with her makeup.

'Good luck then.' Kelley opened the door to see Carl lounging in the passage outside.

He smiled, gesturing towards the ladies' room. 'Girl talk, eh?'

Kelley didn't answer and made to pass him. He grabbed her arm.

'What've you been saying to her?' he hissed. She looked into the cold eyes and a tremor went through her. But she disguised her apprehension and pulled away.

'I was saying she doesn't have to put up with a rat like you,' she said clearly.

The door at the end of the passage opened and Mick Gamble was there, camera raised. The flashbulb popped and he was gone before any of them had time to react. With a roar of rage, Carl followed. The girls looked at each other in dismay and made their way back to the restaurant. Kelley was shaking when she sat down and Marie looked at her anxiously.

'What's going on?' she asked. 'Why was Carl chasing Mick?'

Kelley couldn't speak and Paul's lips set in an angry line. 'Did he upset you?' he asked.

'It's nothing, really. But I'd like to leave if you don't mind.' She was more shaken than she cared to admit.

'Of course. I'll take you home,' Paul said. He waved a hand at their companions. 'It's OK, stay and finish your meal. I'll look after her.'

As they reached the door, Carl stormed past them on his way back to the table. 'Poor Mick,' Paul said. 'Hope Roche didn't catch up with him.'

Outside the restaurant, he waved down a passing taxi. On the way Kelley told him what had happened in the ladies' and how Mick had seized the opportunity to use his camera. In an attempt at nonchalance, she said, 'You know what they say in show business — any publicity is good publicity.'

Paul frowned. 'Don't say that. It's good publicity you need.'

'Don't worry about it. I'm not. Anyway your story will appear soon. As Marie told you, we start shooting soon — Monday — then we'll be ready to go public.'

Paul nodded thoughtfully. 'Trouble is, us newspaper men can turn the most trivial event into good copy. Mick will find an angle I'm sure.' He shrugged and grinned at her. 'I hope you gave Dawn tit for tat.'

Kelley smiled back. 'Actually, I felt sorry for her.'

The taxi turned into a cul-de-sac and stopped in front of a tall Victorian house. Kelley looked up in surprise. 'I thought you were taking me back to Marie's,' she said.

'I will if you want me to. But I hoped you'd come in for a coffee first. There's something I want to show you.'

'All right — just coffee. But I do have an early start tomorrow.'

'So have I — off to Manchester to cover a gig.' He paid off the taxi and led her up the steps to the front door. The flat was at the top of the house, up three flights of uncarpeted stairs. 'Home sweet home. Not much to look at, is it?' he said as he opened the door and switched on the light.

'You're very well organised,' she said, indicating the desk by the window with its neat stacks of files.

'It's not usually like this,' he confessed, bending to turn on the gas fire. 'Sit down. I'll make that coffee.'

Kelley sat in one of the armchairs flanking the fireplace. From behind her in the kitchen alcove she heard Paul filling the kettle, and the rattle and chink of crockery. The butterflies in her stomach were in full flight now and she began to wish she hadn't accepted his invitation.

'I can't stay long,' she said.

'Just a cup of coffee while you read my article. I don't usually let my subjects see a preview.' He put two mugs down on the small table and went over to his desk. 'This is just a rough draft,' he said, handing her several sheets of printout.

'Where are you going to send this?' she asked.

'I've actually done two versions. One is for a Sunday magazine supplement, the other is for a women's magazine.'

As Kelley settled back in the chair and started to read, Paul cradled his mug in both hands, pacing the small room impatiently while she read.

When she'd finished she looked up with a smile. 'This is brilliant,' she said. 'I like the first one best. You've managed to imply that Carl was to blame for me leaving showbiz without actually saying so. Very clever.' She put the sheaf of papers on the table and picked up her mug of coffee.

'I felt I could go to town with that one, be a little more sensational. The women's mag just wanted a straightforward successful businesswoman-type story. But I've still managed to get in a few swipes at the people who wouldn't employ you.' Paul came and squatted beside her. He took her hand. 'You do realise what this means, don't you, Kelley? Once these appear, the other papers will pick up on it. And they'll find their own angle. They won't all be kind to you.'

'I know, but it's a chance you have to take in this business. And after all, it's only a television series. The person behind it all isn't that important, as long as people enjoy watching it.' She finished her coffee and put the mug down. Paul was still holding her other hand and she tried to pull away. He was very close to her. She could see the fine lines at the corners of his eyes and the faint sheen of sweat on his top lip. She smelt the sharp citrus fragrance of his aftershave as she took a deep breath.

He was smiling that warm, tender smile. 'I know we agreed to be just friends. But I want you to stay — and I think you want it too.' He leaned forward and kissed her gently, and with that kiss all her reservations melted away. Her arms came round him and she returned his kiss with a passion that surprised both of them.

He stood up and took her hand, leading her towards the bed. On the way he turned out the overhead light and switched on a shaded bedside lamp. For a long time afterwards the silence was broken only by their breathing and the hiss of the gas fire. Kelley's experience with Carl had left her unprepared for the feelings Paul aroused in her. With her former lover it had been he who led the way and she'd done everything she could to please him without thought of her own gratification.

Paul was tender and considerate, his only thought of her and how, together, they could reach heights of passion she'd never dreamed of.

'I didn't know it could be like this,'

she whispered as Paul stroked her hair and kissed her neck.

'It's called love,' he said. 'I loved you from the first moment I saw you. Say you feel the same way — please.'

'I do. I love you, Paul.' She kissed him again and a little tremor went through her. How did she know it was really love? She'd thought she was in love with Carl and look what happened. But this was different.

Paul leaned on his elbow, looking down on her, his brown eyes concerned. 'I know what a hard time you had, getting over Carl. I've been through it too. And starting another relationship isn't easy. But I won't push you — we'll take things slowly. Just remember I'm here for you.'

A wave of tenderness washed over her. Whatever happened, she knew Paul would never treat her badly the way Carl had. She sighed and settled back into his arms.

★   ★   ★

Kelley sat up, disoriented for a moment, blinking round at the strange room. As the events of the night before flooded back, a warm glow washed over her. But where was Paul? The distant sound of running water reassured her. Then she realised what had woken her. The printer on the table under the window was chattering, spewing out reams of paper. Paul had been at work already.

Glancing at her watch, Kelley gave a gasp. She'd be late for her meeting. Simon was bringing the location finder to Harry's office this morning to show her the photographs he'd taken. As she leapt out of bed, Paul came in from the adjoining bathroom, a towel round his waist, his hair gleaming damply.

He grinned. 'Come on, lazybones. I thought you were a working girl.'

She smiled at him. 'I'd rather stay here,' she said.

'So would I, so don't tempt me.' He came over and kissed her. 'Now, go and shower while I cook breakfast.'

The tiny bathroom was very basic but Paul had thoughtfully put out a clean towel and a bottle of supermarket shampoo. She showered and rubbed her hair almost dry, finger-combing it into some semblance of her usual style and wishing for a hairdryer. Her eyes in the mirror sparkled; the tired, drawn look of recent months was gone. Her skin glowed and she thought the lack of a few amenities a small price to pay for the happiness she felt right now.

'I ought to go home and change,' she said, emerging from the bathroom. 'I'm not suitably dressed for a business meeting.' Her silk suit of the night before was crumpled and her blouse had a wine stain on it.

'You look wonderful to me. But don't worry, I'll drop you off at Marie's.'

She glanced across at the printer. 'What have you been up to while I was sleeping?' she asked.

'I had to finish something I should have done last night,' he said with a grin. 'But I had better things to do.'

Kelley felt herself blushing and Paul said in a hesitant voice, 'You don't regret it — last night?'

She didn't answer straight away. It had been wonderful and she didn't regret it all, but she was still a little confused. They'd spoken of love but then Paul had said they could take things slowly; she needn't feel committed. Did that mean he didn't want commitment either? Did he think she was the kind of girl who would sleep with a man without it? She didn't know what to say but in the end she had to be honest.

She turned to him with a smile. 'No, I don't regret a thing.'

'I'm glad,' Paul said.

Before he could say any more, she put on her jacket and picked up her handbag. 'I must go. This meeting's very important.'

But when she met up with Harry and Simon later that morning she couldn't concentrate as she dreamily re-lived the wonderful night spent in Paul's arms.

22

When Kelley entered Harry's office, she couldn't stop thinking about Paul. Last night had been wonderful. But she wondered if they were going too fast. Perhaps it was as well he was going away for a few days. It would give her time to think. At least he seemed to understand that she was busy with setting up Kelley's Eye. It was just an excuse really. Her experience with Carl had left her feeling so insecure. Was a new relationship so soon a step too far?

Harry didn't give her time to collect her thoughts but seized both her hands and kissed her exuberantly on both cheeks.

'I've had a call from the BBC,' he said. 'They're definitely interested in *Nore Bay* and — guess what? A company in Norway is keen. They buy loads of British programmes apparently.

I'm seeing the BBC chap early next week and we're going to set up a deal to sell it on, once the first series has been shown over here.'

She was so excited that thoughts of Paul vanished and she got out her diary to make a note of the meeting. 'I'll be down in Sussex all next week,' she said. 'I suppose I could come back. Do you really need me?'

'Not so long as you trust me, love. I'll get the best deal I can. You know me, I can get blood out of a stone.' Harry coughed and wheezed as he laughed and lit up another cigar. 'These things'll be the death of me,' he said, waving the smoke away.

Kelley wrinkled her nose. She'd never liked the smell of cigars but she put up with it for Harry. She waved the smoke away and said, 'Of course I trust you. I don't understand all the finance anyway. And I wouldn't have got this far without your backing. So I'll leave you to sort out the details.'

Harry coughed again and grinned.

'Working on this project has given me a new lease of life. The old business practically runs itself and I was getting bored, almost ready to pack it in. Now I'm back to what I do best, wheeling and dealing, so I should be thanking you.' He got up and came round his desk to give her a hug.

Simon turned up later that morning with yet another list of things to do, his hair wilder than ever, his glasses even more uncontrollable. Today, however, he was smiling broadly.

'We've done it, pet,' he announced.

'Done what?' Kelley asked.

'We've found the perfect location.'

Bearing in mind that location shooting was one of the more expensive parts of the production, Kelley had tried to keep the outdoor scenes to a minimum. She hoped that if the series proved popular and they made enough money, she could be more ambitious with any future series. But *Nore Bay*, set in a small fishing town, and chronicling the lives of the inhabitants, depended for its atmosphere on the location.

'Where?' Kelley asked.

'Whitstable on the north Kent coast. And it's got everything — a walled harbour, fishing fleet, quaint little pubs, narrow streets and alleys. It's perfect.'

'You're a genius, Simon,' Kelley beamed, hugging him.

'My location finder is the genius, pet.' Simon tried to sound modest. But he was pleased. He put his arm round Kelley's shoulders. 'We'll have to go down and check it out, but it sounds just right.'

They sat down at the desk with Harry and went through Simon's list. At last they sat back, self-congratulatory smiles on their faces.

'That's it then. We start shooting in Holton next week,' Kelley said.

Simon left and Harry picked up the phone. While he was speaking, Kelley picked up a newspaper from a small table by the window.

As she turned the page she gasped. There was the picture Mick Gamble had taken the evening before. She stood there, fists clenched, while it was clear that Dawn had been crying. Carl hovered in the background, smiling.

But it was the headline which made her stomach churn: '*WILDCAT STARS FIGHT OVER PRODUCER*'.

The story which followed was nowhere near the truth.

'Television producer Carl Roche looked on as former lover Kelley Robinson and current squeeze Dawn Fairley almost came to blows last night in a confrontation in Patti's, the Soho restaurant frequented by media personalities.

Sinking into a chair, her hands shaking, Kelley studied the photograph again. The story went on to re-hash some of the stories that had recently been circulating. Harry must have read this but he hadn't mentioned it. Perhaps he'd hoped she wouldn't see it.

Harry finished his phone conversation and took the paper away. 'Don't let it get to you, love. It's trash anyway.'

'But it wasn't like that,' Kelley wailed.

'Your real friends know that. As for the rest — who cares?' He gave her shoulder a squeeze.

But Kelley couldn't forget it. As she made her way to the station, she found her thoughts returning again and again to the tabloid story and its distasteful innuendoes. Against her will she remembered how Paul had quizzed her about what had happened. She couldn't believe he'd had anything to do with it. But he was friends with Mick and they often worked together. Despite herself, his comment about newspapermen always looking for a good story came back to her. Was that why he'd been so nice to her?

She blinked back tears, feeling betrayed. *I don't seem to be very wise in my choice of men*, she thought, giving herself a mental shake. Perhaps she should concentrate on her career and give up on romance.

23

The filming of the first episode of *Nore Bay* was going well but Kelley's private life was not. She still often thought about Paul and had been tempted to phone him in the past few weeks. But usually she was so exhausted when she got back to the cottage, she just couldn't cope with speaking to him. Besides, he'd phone her if he really wanted to see her again.

That morning she was woken by the wind. Hard drops of rain rattled against the window but the storm didn't last long. It was still blustery though, and as she reached the top of Bury Hill the wind buffeted the car so that it was a struggle to control the wheel. She was glad they'd put off the location shooting till later in the month. Maybe by then the weather would have improved.

At the studio, Simon and most of the

crew had already arrived. It was still early but they couldn't wait to pick up where they'd left off the day before.

Simon was plotting each character's place in the scene they were shooting today. Kelley watched him, marvelling at his intense concentration. He seemed unmoved by the bustle going on around him as the cameraman checked his angles and levels of sound. People were shifting scenery and the actors were milling around them. It all looked so chaotic but, at a word from Simon, everyone took their places and the walkthrough began.

As Kelley went into the little cubbyhole of an office to work on the next episode, the phone rang. It was Marie berating her for not ringing back. 'You've had your mobile switched off so I left a message on your machine. Is everything all right down there?'

'Sorry. I didn't check my messages last night and you know we don't allow mobiles on set. Was it something urgent, Marie?'

'Not really. It's just Paul's back from up north and he's been trying to get hold of you. Something about a story he's doing. He said he'd left a message and wondered if you were still at the cottage or staying in Holton with the rest of the crew. Shall I give him your mobile number?'

'No, don't do that.' Kelley's voice was sharp, almost panic-stricken.

'Why, what's wrong? I thought you two were . . . ' Marie hesitated.

'No, we're not,' she said sharply, a pang of guilt stabbing at her. She'd had time to re-think her hasty assumption that Paul had betrayed her. But she'd left it so long. And he hadn't been in touch with her either.

'Sorry, Marie, but I'm just so busy right now with filming. I haven't got time for — you know. I'll ring him when I'm free.' Kelley had never told Marie how betrayed she felt, how she suspected Paul had been using her to get a sensational story. She'd made up her mind never to let anyone hurt her again. No more relationships. Just a successful career. That's all she wanted and she wasn't about to discuss it with her well-meaning aunt.

'I'm sorry, Marie. I've got to go.'

She put the phone down, trying to suppress a niggling curiosity about why Paul wanted to get in touch. After that horrible newspaper story, she'd decided to have nothing more to do with him. But perhaps she should have let him explain. Her hand hovered over the phone and she jumped when it rang. She picked it up apprehensively.

It was Angela Roche. 'Marie Winters gave me this number. I haven't heard from you for a while and I wanted to let you know that Carl has asked me to send his stuff on. Do you still want me to send that backup thingy?' Her throaty laugh echoed down the line. 'I've been savouring the thought of his reaction. I only wish I could be there to see his face when he gets his come-uppance.'

Kelley had been so busy lately she'd

almost forgotten their plan to try and ruin Carl. Now she spoke hesitantly. 'Look, Angela, I'm not so sure it's a good idea after all . . .'

'You can't back out now,' Angela interrupted. 'I'll send it off today. I need to get rid of his stuff as I'm having his study redecorated.'

'No.' Kelley felt a superstitious dread that even now, with everything going so well, Carl still had the power to hurt her. Why not let well alone, she thought. 'It's too late. It won't work now,' she protested.

'Why not? He's sure to try using it. He won't believe you could stop him. That's what you wanted, isn't it?'

'It's too complicated. I know when we talked before I said it would work. But he's seen me around with Harry Levinson and Simon Kent and he's sure to have heard about my new company and the series we're making.'

'But has he made the connection between you and Kelley's Eye? Even if he saw you with them he'd think you were auditioning for a part. It wouldn't occur to him that you were the producer and co-director of the show.'

Kelley hesitated. 'I suppose you're right. Everyone's been told not to talk about the storyline. It's part of a publicity stunt to generate interest. And we're using a working title. Unless someone talks out of turn, Carl can't possibly know that the script we're shooting down here is the same as the one on that backup.'

'So what's the problem? You haven't got cold feet, have you?'

'Not really.' Kelley hesitated. But before she could convey her doubts, Angela interrupted.

'You're nervous, understandably so. But he can't hurt you now, Kelley. If he takes the bait, he's the one that'll be in the wrong, and if he doesn't — no harm done. But knowing him, he'll take it all right.' Angela's voice trembled in anticipation of her ex-husband's downfall.

Kelley understood how she felt. She'd felt the same way when they'd sat in Angela's elegant drawing room, plotting together. It had seemed such a good idea at the time. Now, she was surprised to discover that she didn't really care. Her revenge would come from the knowledge that he hadn't beaten her; that she was successful in her own right.

The lengthening silence was broken by Angela's impatient, 'Well, shall we go ahead then?'

Kelley sighed. 'It's up to you, Angela. You're the one with the means to do it. Personally, I don't think we should. We'd only be sinking to his level. But I do understand how you feel.'

'You felt the same way only a few weeks ago. Nothing's changed, has it?'

Kelley remembered seeing him on television recently. Carl's over-confident grin, his falsely sincere voice, had been enough to rekindle the burning desire for vengeance. When she'd fallen in love with Paul it hadn't seemed so important. But then Paul had betrayed her too.

She took a deep breath. 'No, Angela, nothing's changed. Send the stuff off at the end of the week then.'

She put the phone down with a sigh as something she'd read a long time ago came into her mind. It was an old Sicilian proverb — '*Revenge is a season in hell*.' She had the awful feeling that if she was responsible for Carl's downfall, she would feel no satisfaction, only guilt.

Back on the studio floor she tried to immerse herself in the make-believe world of *Nore Bay* and its harbour community, but the fun seemed to have gone out of it now.

* * *

When she arrived back at Rivington, longing for the quiet sanctuary of the cottage, she noticed a car parked at the end of the lane. She didn't take much notice. People sometimes parked there while they walked their dogs. But it was unusual to see anyone after dark.

As she turned to lock the car, a figure loomed out of the dusk and she gasped in fright.

'I didn't mean to startle you, Kelley.' The man stepped into the light and she clutched her chest, breathing heavily.

'Paul, you scared hell out of me. What's the idea, turning up here like this? I don't recall inviting you.' Her voice trembled and she struggled to control herself.

'I'm sorry for scaring you. But you didn't answer my calls, so I had to come. I've e-mailed and texted, left messages on your machine . . . '

'I've got nothing to say to you. I don't know why I let myself be taken in by you.'

'I don't know what you're talking about. What have I done? I thought after those nights together . . . ' He broke off.

'You thought you had another good story, that's what you thought.' Kelley almost choked as tears threatened. 'How could you connive with that slimy Mick Gamble?'

'So that's it.' Paul stepped closer despite her attempts to fend him off. 'I had nothing to do with that story.'

'I don't believe you. You used me, Paul. Remember what you said — 'Newspaper men are always looking for good copy; they'll always find an angle.' I trusted you.' Her voice caught on a sob and she turned towards the door. 'Just go away and leave me alone. You've got your story. That's what you wanted, isn't it?'

Shaking, she went into the cottage and slammed the door. Was that what he really thought? She leaned against the door, waiting for the sound of his car reversing down the lane. Even after it had faded she stood there, knees trembling, fighting back tears. She didn't know what to think. Even as she'd accused him, she'd sensed his genuine puzzlement. Had she got it all wrong yet again?

Despite everything, she realised she loved him and would never regret the night they'd spent together. When he'd appeared so suddenly out of the darkness, her heart had leapt. But her joy had quickly faded. Although she had tried to convince herself he wasn't responsible for that awful tabloid story, she couldn't help remembering his cynical words.

Did she dare to believe him? Would she be opening herself to betrayal again? She couldn't take the chance — not with her new business just taking off. Nothing must stand in the way of its success.

But later, after a bath and a hot drink, as she pored over the script, she couldn't concentrate. The image of Paul standing at her front door, gesturing helplessly as he tried to explain, wouldn't go away. Why was she always so ready to believe the worst? After all, he *had* driven all the way down here to see her. Perhaps she should have let him have his say, she thought. But it was too late now. His angry words as she closed the door on him came back to her. He wouldn't be getting in touch again, she thought bleakly. And she wouldn't contact him either.

24

Marie phoned the next day, berating Kelley for sending Paul away. 'He's really upset,' she said.

'Well, I'm upset too,' Kelley replied. 'I just don't want to talk to him at the moment. Besides, we're going down to Whitstable in a day or two and I don't need the hassle.'

But when she'd put the phone down she had second thoughts. Despite his betrayal, she still couldn't forget the night they'd spent together. Well, she'd get in touch when she got back from Kent, she decided.

*   *   *

Whitstable was a charming little town, just right for the outdoor scenes. The walled harbour and narrow streets and alleyways were picturesque but without that touristy picture-postcard look. It was like stepping back in time fifty years.

The first day's shooting had gone well, but Kelley was silent as they walked along the sea wall towards the hotel, plagued by the nagging worry about what Carl would do when he received her script from Angela. Much as she wanted to get even with him, she was still afraid that he would somehow wreck everything.

The tide was coming in over the mudflats, the setting sun dancing on the ripples. The small boats, which had looked abandoned until now, began to float, bobbing at their moorings. A lone seagull's plaintive cry echoed Kelley's mood. With an effort she shook it off as they reached the harbour wall. 'This location's perfect,' she said, trying to sound positive.

'The weather's perfect too.' Simon laughed as a gust of wind blew his long hair across his face. 'The sea's just choppy enough to give a bit of movement to the boats, but not so rough that the cast will be seasick. It would be just our luck to have a dead calm just as we were ready to start shooting.'

'It may be perfect for the film, but I'm freezing. Let's go back.'

★   ★   ★

Simon was right about the weather and they were able to wrap up the location shooting within a few days. Back in Holton they were ready for the next stage of production.

As she watched Simon at work, Kelley realised she still had a lot to learn. She was only just beginning to understand camera movement and lighting and there was the editing to do yet.

She thanked Simon for his patience. 'When I first started, I thought directing was just telling the actors what to do,' she confessed.

'Oh no, pet. You have to understand

every aspect of film. It's all equally important, see. Performance and dialogue are just a part of the whole.' His eyes gleamed behind his glasses as he launched into his favourite subject.

Kelley smiled. His enthusiasm was contagious. *That's why he's so good*, she thought. He projected that enthusiasm. 'I'm still a novice as far as directing goes,' she said.

'But you're getting there. You've got what it takes — I can tell.'

Kelley glowed. His approval meant a lot to her.

She looked round the studio — her studio. Most of the cast and crew had left. Only the clapper loader was still working, cleaning his camera and lenses ready for the next day's shooting.

She was amazed at what she'd achieved in such a short time and felt a lurch in her stomach at the thought that things could still go wrong. But she had to think positively. People were depending on her for their living now, and even Marie and Harry would expect a return on their investment at some time in the future. There was still a long way to go before *Nore Bay* was shown. And she still hadn't an inkling what Carl was up to. What if he hadn't taken the bait, but was hatching his own little plot? The thought brought a chill to her spine.

The clapper loader had finished and Simon shrugged into his jacket and followed him to the door. 'You can't stay here all night, Kelley,' he said. 'Come and have a drink with Jim and me.'

'No thanks. I've got chores to do back at the cottage. See you in the morning.'

As she got into her car she checked her mobile for messages, feeling unreasonably disappointed that Paul hadn't tried to contact her. But then, it was really up to her, wasn't it?

* * *

Carl slammed the phone down furiously. How had he managed to stay

275

calm throughout the BBC producer's stumbling apology? Apparently, *Going Home* hadn't proved as popular as *Land Girls* and the producer regretted he was unable to commission a further series. Viewers had been disappointed when Violet had been killed off, he said, and the substitution of a new character played by Dawn Fairley hadn't filled the void left by Kelley.

Kelley! Carl grabbed a bottle and glass. Nothing had gone right for him since he'd met her. She wasn't like the other girls he'd seduced, and if there was one thing he couldn't tolerate it was a woman with a mind of her own. The idea for the sequel had been hers, but he shouldn't have listened to her. He conveniently forgot how eagerly he'd used her notes and script. She'd let him down, just like all the others.

As he paced the room, all the frustration and anger of the past year welled up in him and he longed to break something, somebody. If Kelley was here, he'd . . .

He raised the whisky glass to his lips and, realising it was empty, splashed more liquid into it. He slumped into a chair, gazing morosely out at the river.

This wasn't about losing money. He'd already made enough to last him several lifetimes. But he did care about losing his place at the top of the ratings. He'd enjoyed the power and the adulation. Kelley was to blame for everything — even the failure of the new series he'd just directed. *Property Ladder*, the script he'd stolen, just hadn't taken off in the way he'd hoped.

He went into the bathroom, swilling his mouth with cold water to get rid of the sour whisky taste, wincing as he noticed the veins threading his cheeks, and the new grey streaks in his hair. Best not to dwell on it, he thought. Work was the antidote to all this soul-searching. He slammed out of the flat and went downstairs to the studio.

Two shows had bombed in the past year and there was nothing to take their place. He'd have to come up with something to put himself back on top, he told himself, contemplating the pile of unsolicited manuscripts that littered his office desk. Then Kelley and Angela, and even Dawn, could go to hell.

He ploughed through the heap of folders. Most of them were rubbish and he piled them into a cardboard box with a note to his secretary to send them all back.

He turned to the letters in his tray and pulled out a package that he hadn't bothered to open earlier. He tipped the contents out, unfolding the single sheet of blue headed notepaper.

'As you requested I dumped your stuff, but I thought this might be important,' Angela had written.

Carl picked up the memory stick. It wasn't labelled and he wondered where it had come from. Probably an unsolicited script, he thought, but considering the dearth of new projects lately it might be worth taking another look. He didn't remember it and his curiosity was aroused. He slipped it into the USB port, drumming his fingers impatiently while he waited for the menu to appear. Then he logged on to the list of files.

'What's this, then?' he said as the title page came up on the screen — '*Nore Bay* by Kelley Robinson.' Bloody Kelley again, he thought. Probably another of her crappy attempts at script-writing. Still, he might as well read it. Maybe he could use it.

His pulse quickened. This was what he'd been looking for, an idea for a new series that might restore his failing fortunes. It wasn't a fully realised script, just a couple of scenes and a story outline. But it had everything — characters, plot, setting. It was just perfect. The only problem was, it had her name on the title page.

He sat back in his chair, drumming his fingers on the desk. Of course he could approach Kelley, tell her he wanted to use her idea and offer her a one-off payment. It would need a lot of work before it got to the screen so she couldn't expect much. At least that's what he'd tell her.

But why bother? He'd do what he'd done before — use the material as if it were his own. Kelley would never have the guts to tackle him about it and she couldn't prove it was her work. After all, it was on an unlabelled backup and had been written while she'd been working for him. How else had it got among his things and been left down at Lydford?

His fingers hovered over the keyboard. Carefully he deleted the words 'Kelley Robinson' and inserted 'Carl Roche'. He smiled. This one would surely wipe out the failures of the past months.

'Thanks, Kelley love. What would I have done without you?' he murmured.

25

The first episode of *Nore Bay* was finished, edited down to the last frame. Kelley was euphoric. Now they had to wait for the public's reaction, but it would be a long wait. The series wouldn't be transmitted until early next year.

'But the BBC's convinced they have a winner on their hands and they're already talking about a second series,' Harry said enthusiastically. They'd returned to his office after signing the contracts and, as usual, he'd lit up a cigar. His doctor had told him to cut down but he could never resist an excuse. Both Kelley and Marie had given up trying to remonstrate with him.

Kelley moved to the window away from Harry's smoke. She felt sad that her parents weren't there to share her excitement that her dreams had come true. They would have been so proud, she thought, swallowing a lump in her throat.

Paul, too, would be pleased for her and she wished she hadn't left it too late to contact him. But she felt so ashamed of the way she'd reacted, not trusting him or giving him a chance to explain. Besides, he hadn't made the slightest attempt to call her. She didn't blame him. He was right to be angry after the way she'd treated him. She wondered if he'd sent the articles to the magazines as he'd promised. She really needed the publicity now. Surely he wouldn't be so petty as to go back on his word, she thought. He was too much of a professional.

She couldn't stop thinking about him and remembering that wonderful night they'd spent together. It could have been the first of many if she hadn't been so paranoid. She sighed and turned away from the window, realising that she hadn't heard a word Harry said.

'Do you realise what this means?' he asked, waving his cigar at her. Fortunately he answered his own question, seeming not to realise that she hadn't been listening. 'An ongoing series, twice a week. We could run as long as *Coronation Street*. That's what they want — good family entertainment. Kelley, darling, if it takes off, you're made.' He planted a kiss on her cheek. 'Come on, let's go and tell Marie.'

'I'm sorry, Harry. I've got to get back to Sussex this afternoon. Lots to do. Tell Marie we'll get together at the weekend.'

'She'll be upset,' Harry warned. 'We'd planned to go out tonight.' But he let her go without pressing the point.

On the train home, Kelley felt depressed, though she should have been on top of the world. She should have taken up Harry's invitation. She hated upsetting him — her aunt too. But she didn't fancy facing either Paul or Carl if they turned up at Patti's. She couldn't wait to get back to the cottage where she could be miserable in peace.

But her spirits lifted when she saw the thick envelope on the doormat. Recognising Paul's flowing scrawl on the label, she tore it open. It contained two magazines with a yellow post-it note stuck on the front of one. 'Hope you approve. Best wishes — Paul'. That was all, but it was enough to send her heart soaring. He couldn't still be mad at her.

Not bothering to take off her jacket, she spread them on the kitchen worktop and flipped through the pages. The first article, in a weekly women's magazine, was a straightforward businesswoman's success story. But Paul had pulled out all the stops in the showbiz article, making much of her determination to overcome the setback of losing a star part, just when her acting success seemed assured.

She read with growing admiration for Paul's skill with words. It was nothing like the sleazy gossip that had been written about her in the tabloids.

A smile curved her lips. He'd done her proud. And now she had an excuse for getting in touch with him. She'd phone straight away and thank him.

She hung her jacket up, slipped her shoes off and went into the living room. The light on the answer phone was blinking and she pressed the button. It was Paul.

'Kelley, I've been trying to get hold of you — couldn't get you on your mobile so I hope you pick this up. Ring me as soon as you can. It's really important. I think Carl's out to get you. We must try to stop him.'

What now? Kelley hastily keyed in Paul's number but there was no reply. She left a voicemail message and a text, then paced the room, returning to the phone to try again — and again. Her stomach churned. What was Carl up to? Her desire for revenge had long since cooled. She'd begun to hope that Angela, too, had realised how foolish their plan was. Had she gone ahead with it? If so, Kelley now feared that the consequences would be as bad for her as she'd hoped they would be for her former lover.

26

Kelley had spent a sleepless night worrying about Paul's message. It was barely light when she tried to ring him again. Still no reply. She left another voicemail.

She felt a cold hand in the pit of her stomach. She'd always known she couldn't beat Carl. It had been her idea, yes, but why had she let Angela talk her into going through with it? Now he could ruin everything, just as she'd always feared. Her first instinct was to rush back to London and confront him, but she knew that wouldn't do any good.

When she reached the studio in Holton, Simon handed her a recorded delivery letter and went to make coffee. She went pale and sat down abruptly. She hardly noticed when he came back with two steaming mugs, her attention on the thick, creamy yellow pages. 'Look what he's done,' she said, thrusting the letter at him.

He set the mugs on the desk and took it. He read it quickly and handed it back, putting his arm round her. 'Don't be upset, pet. No one's going to believe this sort of rubbish.'

'Upset? Why shouldn't I be upset?' She shook off his comforting arm. 'I'm bloody furious. How dare he accuse me?'

'It's a bit much, getting his solicitor to write to you. How does he think he'll get away with it? Our series is in the bag and he's only just started on his. He hasn't a leg to stand on.'

'This must be what Paul was warning me about. He said Carl was up to something.' She didn't dare tell Simon that it was all her own fault.

'Did you ever discuss the idea for *Nore Bay* with him?' Simon asked and, ignoring Kelley's positive shake of the head, he went on, 'It could be a genuine misunderstanding — especially as we kept it all quiet. He mightn't have realised what we were working on.'

'I never said a word to him, not after the other times. He promised me a credit for *Going Home* but I didn't get it. And when he did *Property Ladder* he didn't even have the decency to consult me. They were both my ideas and I did a lot of work on them.' Kelley looked at Simon accusingly. 'Even you didn't believe me when I told you about it. And now he's accusing me.'

'I'm sorry, pet. I realise now . . . '

Kelley shook her head. 'Water under the bridge. Harry convinced me it would do no good to take it further.' She stood up, pacing the room. 'I tell you, Simon, *Nore Bay* was all my own work. He couldn't have known anything about it.'

'So how did he get hold of it then?' Simon asked. 'Did you leave it in his flat? He probably thought you'd forgotten about it.'

Kelley almost blurted out the truth, but she didn't think Simon would understand. *I might have known Carl would turn the tables on me,* she thought. But he wouldn't get away with it.

Angrily she pounded the desk. 'I swear to you, Carl had nothing to do with it.' Despite the fact that she'd practically handed the script to him on a plate and he'd done precisely as she'd originally planned, she couldn't control her anger. The arrogance of the man. He'd stolen her work and then accused *her* of plagiarism. 'I'll fight him all the way,' she said, glaring at Simon.

Poor Simon — it wasn't his fault. She apologised and he smiled sympathetically.

'I know how hard you've worked,' he said. 'You'd better ring Harry. Perhaps he can help.'

'Thanks, Simon, for believing me. Anyway, we've still got the show. He can't sabotage that now — can he?' she asked, a pleading note in her voice.

★ ★ ★

As a director of Kelley's Eye Productions, Harry had received an identical letter from Carl's solicitor that morning. 'Oh, no. She's gone and done it,' he groaned aloud. 'Wish she'd discussed it with me first.' He sighed and lit up a cigar. Good as he'd feel to see the Cockroach get his come-uppance, he'd become increasingly doubtful about whether it was worth the hassle. And, as Kelley hadn't mentioned it recently, he'd hoped she felt the same way.

Confident that *Nore Bay* would be a brilliant success, he felt that Roche would soon be a has-been anyway. His shows were slipping from the ratings and others were scrambling to take his place. Surely that was revenge enough for Kelley.

Now, with the solicitor's letter in his hand, he realised Roche wouldn't go down without a fight. Chewing furiously on his cigar, he wondered how they'd get out of this mess without Kelley being hurt. Well, he had the memory stick which proved when she'd started work on *Nore Bay*. But would that be enough?

'What a mess,' he muttered round the chewed end of his cigar. He should have talked her out of it. But in the hectic preparations for launching their company, he really hadn't given it another thought.

He was still pacing the room when she phoned. Doing his best to calm her down, he suggested she come to London on the next train. 'We'll see my solicitor and find out where we stand,' he said.

He got out copies of Kelley's contract. She'd only been employed as an actress, but there might be something in the small print about any scripts she developed while working at River View being their property. Roche could make use of that to build a case against her. Of course, she'd left by the time she started work on *Nore Bay*. But who would believe her?

Harry was immersed in paperwork when Paul knocked on the door. *Oh*

God, reporters. That's all I need, he thought, removing the cigar to give the young man a cursory greeting.

'No stories for you today, mate. Sorry.'

'That's not what I'm after. I need to contact Kelley. I've left messages but she hasn't got back to me,' Paul said.

'She's down in Sussex.' Harry was reluctant to say more. He knew Kelley had fallen out with him. He didn't want to upset her, especially now. She'd have enough to worry about dealing with the Cockroach.

'Harry, I must speak to her. I've heard Carl Roche is out to get her,' Paul said.

Studying the chewed end of his cigar thoughtfully, Harry tried to decide if Paul was genuinely concerned about Kelley. Was he just looking for a story? That was the trouble with journalists, you never knew if they were trying to trick you into being indiscreet. But Paul had never let him down in the past — 'off the record' really did mean just that. And if he really cared for Kelley, well, she needed all the friends she could get.

However, he thought it best not to say that she was on her way to London. Compromising, he said, 'I expect to hear from her soon. I'll tell her to ring you.'

Paul leaned over the desk and shook Harry's hand. 'Thanks, I owe you.'

I believe he really is sweet on the girl, Harry thought with a grin as Paul slammed the door and clattered down the stairs.

★　★　★

Kelley was paying off the taxi and fighting to open her umbrella when she turned and caught sight of Paul. Her heart lurched and she smiled, unable to hide her pleasure at seeing him.

Before she could speak, he grabbed her arm. 'Kelley, thank God I've caught up with you at last. I need to talk to you. Didn't you get my message?'

'I've been trying to contact *you*,' she said. 'But do you think you could say 'hello' first?'

He ran his fingers through his wet hair. 'Sorry. It's just — I've been so worried.'

'Thanks, Paul, but I know what it's about, though I can't think how you knew. I only got the letter this morning. Must be your journalist's instinct for a story.'

He groaned. 'Kelley, don't let's go through all that again. I thought when you got the magazines you'd realise I'm on your side. I wouldn't do anything to hurt you.

'I'm sorry too — for doubting you, for refusing to listen when you came down to the cottage . . . '

'Let's start again, shall we? I'm your friend and I want to help. Will you let me?'

She nodded. 'Come up to Harry's office and I'll tell you what's been going on.' She grinned mischievously. 'Off the record?'

'Off the record,' he agreed, laughing and taking her hand.

Harry leapt up when they entered the office. 'You again,' he growled. 'Don't say anything, Kelley. He's already been here once today, asking questions, trying to find out what's going on.'

'It's OK, Harry. Paul's on our side. He won't publish anything unless we agree. And he may be able to help.'

'You've changed your tune, girl.' Harry sat behind his desk, waving them to chairs opposite. They hung their wet coats up behind the door and Harry picked up his copy of the letter. 'We can't ignore this. I've made an appointment with Jack Brinsley, my solicitor.'

Kelley looked anxious and Paul reached for her hand. She held on to it gratefully, turning to smile at him.

'First, we'd better get our facts right,' Harry continued. 'Are you sure you didn't discuss *Nore Bay* at all while you were still living with Carl? If so, he could claim it was a joint project.'

'I didn't talk to him about it at all'

Kelley said positively.

'Good. I've checked your contract with River View and it only refers to acting. There's nothing to say you couldn't do other work while you were with them. So it looks like we're OK.'

'But you know I'd already left *Land Girls* when I wrote it.' Kelley stopped and bit her lip. This was awful. She couldn't bear Paul finding out how she'd tricked Carl. Anyway it was all Angela's fault, she thought. But in all honesty, it had been her idea and she only had herself to blame for the mess she was in. It was Paul's reaction that worried her. Would he recoil in disgust when he realised what a nasty, vindictive person she was?

His words almost echoed Simon's earlier. 'So, how did Carl manage to get hold of your script?'

Kelley withdrew her hand and went over to the window. It would be easier to speak truthfully if they weren't face to face. 'It's my own fault really,' she began hesitantly. 'I suppose I didn't

297

think it through properly. I was so angry with Carl, I just wanted to get back at him.'

Paul remained silent and Kelley turned to face him.

'I went to see Carl's wife — we hatched a plot to discredit him. She was even more keen than I was.' Kelley broke off with a sigh, glancing at Harry for support.

'Go on, love. You might as well tell him the rest,' Harry said.

'What did you do, Kelley? I don't understand,' Paul said.

Kelley took a deep breath and explained how they'd tricked Carl into using her script.

She avoided his eyes, feeling ashamed now. 'I was angry — with myself too. I just wanted to fight back.' She paused and looked down at her hands. 'Once I realised *Nore Bay* was going to be a success, I didn't care about Carl anymore. Getting my own back didn't seem so important.'

'What happened?' Paul asked quietly.

'I forgot all about it until Angela rang me. I told her I wasn't sure about going ahead, but she got me all worked up again. She sent the memory stick and Carl took the bait.'

She sat down, keeping a distance between herself and Paul, not looking at him. *I've blown it now*, she thought. *I bet he's thinking 'What a story.'*

But when he spoke, there was a hint of laughter in his voice. 'Remind me never to get on your wrong side,' he said.

She dared to meet his eyes. To her relief, he was smiling. He couldn't think too badly of her then. She couldn't smile back though. 'I never meant it to go this far, and cause all this trouble,' she wailed. 'What are we going to do?'

'Well, for a start I think Jack will suggest we put in a counter claim. Obviously Roche is the plagiarist,' Harry said. 'When he sees the evidence that you wrote the script *after* you'd split up, he'll probably cave in.'

'What evidence?' Paul asked.

'I've got a copy in my safe, labelled, signed and dated.'

'That should do it,' Paul said.

But Kelley was still doubtful. 'He's going to realise I tricked him. How else could Angela have got hold of it? Suppose he tries something else?'

Paul laughed. 'Knowing Carl, he won't want to broadcast that a mere woman tried and almost succeeded in getting the better of him. A quiet hint that the press might get hold of the story should do the trick. I don't think he'll bother you again.

'Let's wait and see what Jack says first,' Harry said, leaning back in his chair and lighting another cigar. 'What gets me is the sheer nerve of the man. He develops your script and tries to pass it off as his own. But when he realises you've beaten him to it, he accuses you of doing the very same thing.'

'He's had his own way for too long. He thinks he can get away with anything,' Paul said.

'But not this time,' Harry said firmly.

Kelley smiled hesitantly. 'You don't think too badly of me, do you? I wasn't thinking straight for a while.'

Paul took her hand. 'I don't blame you for wanting to get back at him. But it's all over now. The solicitor will sort it all out.'

This time Kelley didn't pull away. But she was still worried. 'Will we have to tell Mr Brinsley what I did? I feel so embarrassed. It was a stupid idea.'

Harry thought for a minute. 'We really ought to come clean so he knows what we're up against. But he's probably heard far worse in his time. Don't worry; you're going to come out on top, Kelley love.'

When they left for their appointment with Jack Brinsley, Paul said, 'I think it's best if I let you and Harry see Brinsley alone. He might not like a reporter sitting in.'

'No, you must come too — I need moral support,' Kelley said.

Paul grinned and grabbed his leather jacket off the back of the chair. 'My car's outside,' he said.

Jack Brinsley mopped his face and gleaming pate with a large blue handkerchief and shook Kelley's hand. She tried to look cool but she was horrified at the thought of telling him the whole story.

Harry passed him the letter from Carl's solicitor and Kelley also handed over her copy with the memory stick and her diary containing notes of when she'd started work on *Nore Bay*. Harry also had the copy still in its jiffy bag with the postmark and the recorded delivery slip. The solicitor perused them quickly and began asking questions in a clipped, brisk tone.

As they waited for his conclusions, Kelley realised she was clutching Paul's hand.

When Brinsley finally spoke, he asked, 'How is it possible that Roche stole the memory stick if you didn't start work on it till you'd left London? Are you seriously suggesting he broke into your cottage and took it?'

'I told you, Angela had it. She sent it to him,' Kelley said.

Brinsley mopped his face again and leaned back in his chair, thinking. 'We don't want him to realise you were trying to trick him, so . . . can you think of any reason you'd have gone to see Mrs Roche, other than the real one of course? Did you perhaps hope to confront Roche there?'

'Of course I didn't. Not after what he did to me.'

'I'm sorry, Miss Robinson. But if it should come to a court case, this is the sort of thing Roche's counsel will ask. Now think. Was there a legitimate reason for you to have gone there?'

Harry interrupted. 'You were looking for backing for your series. Angela Roche is a rich woman. Didn't you go to see her, hoping she'd help you financially? If you left the memory stick behind, she could have genuinely believed it belonged to her husband.'

He grinned and Kelley blessed his quick mind.

'Yes, that's it. I'm sure Angela will back me up. That would explain things. And when she sent Carl's things on, he seized the chance to steal yet another of my scripts.'

Brinsley thought for a moment and said, 'What possessed the man to think he'd get away with it?'

'He's an arrogant swine,' Harry said. 'And he thought he'd seen the last of Kelley when she went back to Sussex after her father died.'

Jack Brinsley winced at Harry's forthright tone. 'We must handle this very carefully. In the first instance I'll write to Warren Smith suggesting that his client has made a genuine mistake. Then we'll await developments. Don't worry, my dear, I'm sure we'll sort this out quite quickly.'

Kelley should have been relieved but the solicitor's mention of a court case had left her with a hollow feeling. How would she cope with that? Despite Harry's reassurance, she could imagine what the publicity would do to her and the prospect of a second series of *Nore Bay*.

When they left Brinsley's office, the rain had stopped again and the pavements steamed in the warm, humid air. Paul opened the passenger door of the Volkswagen. 'Where to?' he asked.

'I must get back to the office,' Harry said. 'What are your plans, love?'

'It's too late to go down to Holton now. But if I catch the next train I can stay at the cottage and get to the studio early tomorrow morning.'

'I'll give you a lift to the station — or better still, drive you home. I've got the rest of the day free,' Paul offered.

She hesitated, but Harry said, 'Go on, Kelley. It'll give you two a chance to talk.'

They were silent until they took the sliproad onto the M23, when Paul turned to her and said, 'Don't worry, Kelley. It's going to be OK.'

'Do you really think so?' She didn't want to get her hopes up. Could it possibly all turn out all right?

As they left the motorway and meandered through the winding Sussex lanes, the rain started again. Paul peered through the windscreen and said, 'You'll have to direct me from here. I came a different way last time and got hopelessly lost.'

Kelley didn't want to be reminded of his last visit to Rivington. She couldn't believe how badly she'd behaved. Now she looked at Paul's profile — the long, straight nose, the lock of wavy brown hair falling over his eyes — and her heart turned over. He wasn't as handsome as Carl, but she knew how his mouth could relax in that engaging grin, and his brown eyes grow warm with love and laughter. It had taken a long time for her to realise the difference between love and infatuation.

But dare she reveal her feelings? They were friends again, but did he want more than that? So much had happened since that night at his flat, and she'd been so confused since then.

Should she tell him how she felt and

risk driving him away? Or just settle for friendship and hope he'd come to love her too? He'd been very quiet. Perhaps he was thinking the same thing. She dared to hope and resolved that she would ask him to stay and see what happened.

'Not far now. I think I can remember the way from here,' Paul said. 'You know, I envy you, having this place. It must be great to have somewhere where you can get away from all the hassle.'

'It is. Much as I love the hurly burly of London life, I need to get away occasionally. This is where I do my thinking,' Kelley replied.

They reached the village and Paul slowed down as they drove through the winding street of flint cottages. The front gardens were ablaze with summer flowers, a little battered now by the driving rain. He parked at the end of the lane where he'd left his car before. As he followed Kelley up the front path he gave a little laugh. 'I hope you're not going to slam the door in my face again,' he said. 'It's wet out here.'

She almost made an angry retort, until she noticed the expression in his eyes — a little wary, as if afraid she would indeed send him on his way. Perhaps he was as nervous as she was. She'd have to make the first move if they were ever going to resolve things.

She smiled and opened the door wide. 'Actually, I was going to ask you to stay,' she said.

'For tea? For coffee? Forever?' His joky tone broke the ice and they both laughed.

Kelley's expression grew serious. 'For as long as you want to,' she said.

'Do you mean that?'

She nodded and Paul moved towards her. The kiss that followed said more than words ever could.

When she drew away, she said breathlessly, 'Do you mind if we close the door? This is a quiet little village but there's always someone around.'

Without speaking, Paul kicked the front door shut behind him and took her in his arms again.

Black thunderclouds had built up and it was almost dark in the little living room. As they moved towards the sofa, thunder crashed overhead and lightning split the dark sky. But the storm raging overhead was insignificant, compared to the storm of passion unleashed by that kiss.

★   ★   ★

It was late evening. The cloudburst was over and the lowering sun cast a pink glow through the west facing windows. Kelley stirred and stretched.

Paul was sitting by the window, looking out at the rain-drenched garden. 'I hope you meant that about me staying forever. This is a magic place,' he said.

'It's not the place, it's the people you share it with that make it magic,' she replied, getting up and kissing him.

His arms tightened around her. 'I was going to suggest we went out to eat. But if you keep doing that I really will want to stay here forever,' he said.

Kelley laughed and stepped away. 'I prefer the first suggestion. I'm starving.'

They went to the village pub and ate chilli with fresh crusty bread, pausing frequently to touch hands, smile dreamily and say the silly things that lovers always say. Lingering over their coffee, they suddenly ran out of conversation. Kelley felt so happy, she was reluctant to break the spell. She fiddled with her spoon, staring into her coffee. She couldn't bear it if he decided to go back to London now.

As she hesitated, he leaned towards her and said, 'You are really over him, aren't you?'

'Of course I am. I have been for a long time. What makes you ask now, of all times?' She couldn't hide the hurt tone.

'You got so upset when we were discussing him earlier. I just want to be sure.'

'I was angry, not upset. I don't feel

anything for him at all. In fact, I know now I never really loved him.' She paused and looked straight at him. 'It's you I love, Paul. Even when I accused you of using me, I didn't really believe it. But Carl made me feel so insecure, so useless, I couldn't believe anyone could really love me.'

'Oh Kelley, what a lot of time we've wasted with these silly misunderstandings.' He leaned over and took her hand. 'Come on, I'll pay the bill and then it's back to the magic cottage for a night of enchantment.'

Kelley's face cleared and she laughed aloud. 'You have such a way of putting things. No wonder you're a writer.'

'Clichés — the stock-in-trade of a tabloid hack,' he said, laughing.

'Don't put yourself down, Paul. You're a good writer. You should be concentrating on the serious stuff.'

'I am,' he said. 'I'm writing a book.'

As they strolled back through the village, arms entwined, breathing in the heady smell of summer gardens after

311

rain, he told her about his ambitions. But as they neared the house, they fell silent and their footsteps quickened. They couldn't wait to get inside.

Later, as Paul slept, Kelley watched the progress of the moonlight across the bedroom floor, too happy to sleep. Her worries about Carl were insignificant now.

27

Kelley hadn't felt this nervous since her first audition. How could she face the hatred she was sure she would see in Carl's icy blue eyes? When Rowena had rung to say Bruce Clark wanted her to appear with him on *London Tonight* she'd almost refused. But Rowena said, 'There's a lot of rumours flying around about this new series. It's your chance to tell your side of the story.'

Kelley had given in and now Paul squeezed her hand and urged her onto the set. 'You can do it, darling.'

Once seated on the sofa next to Carl, her nerves fled. Focusing her attention on Bruce, she answered his questions with a serenity that belied her inner trembling.

At first the questions were about Kelley's reasons for leaving the wartime series. Then Bruce came to the nitty-gritty. 'So, Kelley — when you couldn't get any parts you turned your hand to a completely new venture and set up your own production company, Kelley's Eye.'

'That's right. Though at this point I'd like to say I didn't do it all on my own.'

'I'll say,' Carl interrupted.

Bruce gestured at him to wait and encouraged Kelley to go on.

'I was going to say that I had the help of my agent Harry Levinson and my aunt Marie Winters. They both had enough faith in me to invest in my company.'

Bruce nodded and consulted his clipboard. 'This new show of yours, *Nore Bay*? I gather there's been some controversy about the script.'

Before Kelley could answer, Carl interrupted, 'We've already agreed there was a misunderstanding. I didn't come on your show to listen to her calling me a thief.'

Kelley flinched as Carl's voice grew louder but Bruce took control again.

'The question is, Carl: *Did* you steal it? Are you guilty of plagiarizing the work of someone with more talent than yourself?'

'I don't have to listen to this,' Carl roared. He leapt up and lunged towards Kelley. 'You bitch. You set me up. No one does that and gets away with it. You know I'll make you pay for this,' he snarled.

Bruce tried to intervene. But Kelley, drawing on reserves of courage she didn't know she possessed, straightened in her seat. 'I don't think I'm the one who's going to pay,' she said calmly.

Carl's clenched fist came up, then he gave a short laugh, his hand dropped to his side and he stumbled off the set.

Bruce signalled for a break and someone handed Kelley a glass of water. Then Paul rushed onto the set and his arms came round her. 'Well done, darling. You were marvellous, keeping your cool like that.'

After the break, Bruce introduced his other guest, Angela Roche. She backed

Kelley's story and revealed more about her former husband than even Kelley had bargained for.

Afterwards Kelley felt drained. She just wanted to go back to the cottage with Paul. But Harry was waiting for them, looking thoughtfully at the end of his cigar, instead of grinning and planning a celebration as she had expected. 'Why so gloomy? I thought you'd be cracking the champagne or ringing up to book a table at Patti's,' she said.

'I'm getting too old for all these capers,' he replied.

'Nonsense,' Kelley said. But he was looking tired. She'd been so involved with her own troubles that she hadn't noticed. 'What's wrong, Harry?' she asked.

'I'm fed up, that's what's wrong.' He threw the chewed cigar into an ashtray. 'I've got to give these up, and the booze. How can you celebrate without a good cigar and a magnum of the fizzy stuff?' He leaned towards Kelley confidingly. 'You won't tell Marie, will you, love? She worries enough already.'

'What is it, Harry?'

He tapped his chest. 'The doc says I've got to give up the business, too, or else . . .'

Kelley sympathised. Harry loved being in the thick of things and jumped at any excuse for a celebration. He claimed he couldn't think without a cigar to chew on.

'Tell you what, love — we *will* celebrate. One last fling to toast your success. It's time I retired anyway. Go out with a bang, what do you say?'

Kelley nodded. His news had completely driven the recent confrontation with Carl from her mind.

While she and Paul waited for Harry and Marie, Kelley said, 'I hope he's exaggerating. He always dramatises things, so it's hard to tell. I should have noticed something was wrong.'

'You've had a lot on your plate lately. Don't worry, Marie will make him look after himself.'

'But I've promised not to say anything. Maybe I'll suggest they take a

317

holiday,' she said.

'Poor old Harry. It'll come hard, giving up the smoking and drinking. He loves the good life. Do you think he'll do as he's told?'

'I hope so for Marie's sake. I don't know what she'd do without him,' Kelley said. She leaned over and gave Paul a kiss. 'I don't know what I'd do without you either. You've been a rock these last few weeks. I wish we weren't going out tonight. But if it really is Harry's last fling we can't disappoint him, can we?'

'No, of course not. Besides, we've got all the time in the world.'

Kelley kissed him warmly, loving him for caring. It was a long time before they spoke again; they were so wrapped up in each other that they jumped when Harry opened the car door.

★   ★   ★

He'd booked the best table, the one Carl Roche had always looked on as 'his'. The champagne was already on ice and as they came in the maître d' greeted them effusively, drawing the attention of the other diners.

Kelley tried not to feel embarrassed. She'd have to get used to it if things carried on like this. Funny, she thought. She never minded the attention when she was a well-known actress. But then she'd been a different person.

As usual the restaurant was full of media people, and Kelley acknowledged the nods in their direction with a smile. But when Carl came in, she felt that familiar flip in the pit of her stomach. Would he make another scene? She picked up her glass, willing her hand not to tremble. He couldn't hurt her now.

The conversation around them died briefly and Paul took Kelley's hand, squeezing her fingers. 'He can't do anything to you now,' he whispered.

She smiled at him gratefully. 'I'm all right,' she said as Carl passed their table. No young blonde in tow this time. There was nothing there of the man she thought she'd been in love with. His glance swept over her and he joined a group of his loyal cronies at a corner table.

As Kelley ate and drank, she managed to forget that Carl was there. Harry seemed to be a little subdued, but Marie appeared not to notice, laughing heartily when he did an impersonation of Bruce Clark asking Carl that loaded question.

Harry had called for more champagne when there was a commotion in the far corner of the restaurant. Carl had stood up, knocking his chair over. A waiter hovered nearby but Carl waved him away. Spitting an obscenity, he pushed his way between the tables and slammed out, leaving his friends to placate the waiter and pay the bill. After a moment of stunned silence, things in the room returned to normal.

Kelley wondered why she had wasted so much time on such destructive emotions. She'd proved she was capable of running a business using her creative talents, but most importantly, she was loved by a caring, sensitive man. Paul loved her for herself. Unlike Carl, he didn't need to try to mould her into some ideal. At last she could think of her former lover with no trace of the anger and bitterness that had sustained her for so long. A year ago she'd sat here, planning to destroy him, desperate for revenge. But he'd brought about his own downfall by his greed and arrogance. It would have happened sooner or later.

Kelley reached across and took Paul's hand. 'Shall we tell them now?' she asked. Paul nodded and was about to speak when Harry tapped his fork against his glass.

'I have an announcement to make,' he said. 'I thought I would never want to retire. But I've been giving it some thought and I — we've — decided . . . ' He smiled down at Marie. 'I'm going to give up the agency. Oh, I'll still keep my interest in Kelley's Eye, but only in a small way.' He looked at Kelley. 'You don't need me, love, but I'll be at the end of the phone if necessary.'

Kelley hugged him and whispered so that Marie couldn't hear. 'You've decided to be sensible then. I'm so pleased.'

'And that's not all,' Marie interrupted. 'I'm retiring too. Well, not exactly. But I'm letting Cheryl take over as manager of Marie's. She's been practically running the place the past few months anyway.'

'But what are you going to do with yourselves?' Paul asked. 'I can't imagine either of you leading lives of leisure.'

'Well, for starters we're going on a world cruise, finishing up in New Zealand, visiting Marie's brother,' Harry said, pausing to fill their glasses. 'This is the best bit though. It's going to be our honeymoon.' He sat back in his chair, grinning at their surprised expressions.

Kelley looked at Paul and started to laugh. 'Talk about being upstaged at your own celebration,' she said, raising her glass. 'Well, while we're drinking a toast to your future, you'd better drink to ours.' She turned to Paul with a smile. 'Perhaps we could make it a double wedding.'

THE END

We do hope that you have enjoyed reading this large print book.

Did you know that all of our titles are available for purchase?

We publish a wide range of high quality large print books including:
Romances, Mysteries, Classics
General Fiction
Non Fiction and Westerns

Special interest titles available in large print are:
The Little Oxford Dictionary
Music Book, Song Book
Hymn Book, Service Book

Also available from us courtesy of Oxford University Press:
Young Readers' Dictionary
(large print edition)
Young Readers' Thesaurus
(large print edition)

For further information or a free brochure, please contact us at:
Ulverscroft Large Print Books Ltd.,
The Green, Bradgate Road, Anstey,
Leicester, LE7 7FU, England.
Tel: (00 44) 0116 236 4325
Fax: (00 44) 0116 234 0205

VALENTINE MASQUERADE

Margaret Sutherland

New Year's Eve is hot and sultry in more ways than one when a tall, handsome prince fixes the newest lady in his court with a magnetic gaze. Who could say no to a prince — especially a charmer like Will Bradshaw? Caitlin has to wonder. And Will wonders, too, if he might have finally found the woman to banish the hurts of years gone by. But what if the one ill-judged mistake of Caitlin's past happens to be the single fault he can't accept?

THE HOUSE ON THE HILL

Miranda Barnes

When a young man moves into the old house next door, Kate Jackson's curiosity is piqued. However, handsome Elek Costas is suspiciously reclusive, and the two get off to a bad start when he accuses her of trespassing. Whilst Kate is dubious of Elek's claim to be the rightful owner, her boyfriend Robert has his eye on acquiring the property for himself . . . Just what is the mystery of Hillside House? Kate is determined to find out!

THE DUKE'S RELUCTANT BRIDE

Fenella J. Miller

Newly Duke of Hathersage, Colonel Elliott Bromley is obliged to marry one of the old duke's brood in order to release his inheritance. Vivacious and impertinent Lady Rosamond, the second daughter, most definitely wishes to remain a spinster — just five years more and her own inheritance will grant her the independence she needs to establish herself as a novelist. But one of the sisters must wed the new heir to keep the estate in the family — and Elliott has chosen Rosamond . . .

LOVING PROTECTOR

Sally Quilford

En route to London for the Season, Calista Haywood and her family are saved from a highwayman by the dashing Brook Windebank. Later, when he valiantly steps in to prevent an unpleasant earl from claiming Calista as his wife, she fears that Brook is only being chivalrous and will never love her as she loves him. Then, when Brook is attacked and lying close to death, she is forced to pit her wits against his mercurial father, the Duke of Midchester . . .

GETTING A LIFE

Chrissie Loveday

Sick of being the odd one out, lecturer Joanne Swithenbank books an escort to accompany her to the college Christmas formal dinner dance. But 'Rudy' turns out to be Michael Thomas, one of her mature students! Once the dinner is over, she realises she actually likes this man. Could he ever possibly fall for his tutor? Joanne dares to start believing so — until her best friend Trisha sees Michael out with another woman . . .

WILD FRANGIPANI

Wendy Kremer

Katie thinks she's landed a dream job when she travels to the South Pacific island of Naraotoa to manage a hotel. However, her new employer Daniel is an infuriating man who clearly considers her qualifications and experience inadequate. Determined to prove him wrong, Katie settles into her new role, and they even begin to warm to each other — possibly a little too much. For, despite the presence of his gorgeous girlfriend Sharon, Daniel is giving off some extremely flirtatious signals . . .